SMITTEN

WITH BAKLAVA

SMITTEN

WITH BAKLAVA

A SWEET ROMANTIC COMEDY

SET IN GREECE

ELLEN JACOBSON

Smitten with Baklava
Copyright © 2022 by Ellen Jacobson

Print ISBN: 978-1-951495-35-0
Digital ISBN: 978-1-951495-34-3
Large Print ISBN: 978-1-951495-36-7

Editor: By the Book Editing
Cover Design: Melody Jeffries Design

First Printing: November 2022

Published by: Ellen Jacobson
www.ellenjacobsonauthor.com

For everyone out there who's had to eat something they don't like, and then smile and pretend they loved it.

CONTENTS

1	Talking Goats	1
2	Loonies and Toonies	14
3	Going Undercover	31
4	Taco Pajamas	45
5	Hate-Flirting	56
6	Unibrows and Extra Brain Cells	72
7	A Peace Offering	86
8	Another Donkey Ride	98
9	Life Lessons from a Cat	109
10	Human Hairballs	121
11	Strong and Complicated	135
12	Burnt Baklava	145
13	The Goddess of Spring	157
14	Yodeling Brings People Together	168
15	An Unexpected Visitor	178
16	Tacos for the Win	193
	Epilogue – Xander	208
	Author's Note	213
	About the Author	215
	Also by Ellen Jacobson	216

CHAPTER 1
TALKING GOATS

As the ferry makes its way past the brightly painted wooden fishing boats dotting the harbor, I wonder for the millionth time what in the world I'm doing vacationing in Greece. I can't quite wrap my head around the fact that I'm about to spend two weeks on an island in the Aegean Sea doing absolutely nothing. No work emails, no conference calls, no staff meetings, no spreadsheets. Just fourteen days of rest and relaxation.

It sounds dreadful, doesn't it? Believe me, being here wasn't my idea.

Two days ago, my company's HR Director had called me. "Olivia, you have to take at least two weeks of vacation starting next week," she said.

"I'm really sorry, Maria, but it would be impossible

to take a vacation right now," I said. "I'm in the middle of finishing up my current project in Toronto, then I'm due to fly out to Dubai next week."

"No ifs, ands, or buts," she said sternly.

"But—"

Maria interrupted me. "What did I say about 'buts'?"

As I tried to think of another word for 'but,' my stomach churned. My manager, Frank, would flip if I suddenly went on a vacation, especially given the high stakes of the Dubai project. But Maria had been on my case for the past month, warning me that it wasn't healthy to work non-stop for five years without taking time off.

I hate saying no to people. I can't help it. People pleasing is my superpower. I was at a loss. Did I agree to Maria's demand that I take a vacation and infuriate my boss? Or show up in Dubai as scheduled, which would test Maria's patience to no end.

Choosing my next words carefully, I said, "Would it be possible for me to take a vacation after the Dubai project?"

"You said the same exact thing before Toronto, not to mention the Singapore project, the Australia project, the Costa Rica project, and all the other projects you've been assigned to." Maria sighed. "Don't make the same mistake I made. Being so focused on your career, working non-stop, only to find you've turned sixty and all that you have to show for your life is an impressive resume, but nothing else —that's something you'll regret. You're what, twenty-seven, twenty-eight?"

"I'll be thirty next month."

"That's a big milestone, Olivia. It's time you learned about work-life balance before then. Your vacation starts on Monday. End of discussion."

"But . . ."

"No 'buts,'" she reminded me. "Now, I'll take care of Frank. Your only responsibility is to plan where you're going to go to rest and relax. Trust me, you'll thank me afterward."

My shoulders tensed up, thinking about how my manager would react when he heard that I wouldn't be in Dubai as planned. Frank isn't exactly an understanding kind of guy.

"Now, before you start hatching a plan to work remotely while you're on vacation," Maria said with a warning tone in her voice, "you should know that I'm going to remove your access to the company network on a temporary basis. If you even so much as try to send a work-related email or make a work-related call, you'll be on permanent vacation. Understand?"

"Permanent vacation?" My voice squeaked. "As in, you'll fire me?"

"That's what happens when you violate company policy," she said. "And our policy is very clear that employees need to take time off every year. Need I remind you how much unused vacation time you have?"

Someone taps me on the shoulder, interrupting my memories of that agonizing conversation and the HR Director's ultimatum—relax for two weeks or lose my job.

"Do you mind taking a picture of my husband and me?" An older woman with an Australian accent holds out her phone. Her thick silver hair is tied back in a loose ponytail and she's dressed in hiking gear from head to toe. Her husband is attired similarly, clearly ready to hit the trail at a moment's notice.

"Say 'Vegemite,'" I joke as they pose against the railing.

They do a double take, then grin as I take a few photos.

"I can't believe you know what Vegemite is," the woman says as I hand back her phone.

"I spent some time working in Australia," I explain. "My colleagues loved slathering it on their toast in the morning."

"But not you, luv?" she asks.

I repress a shudder. Eating something made out of yeast extract? No thanks, I'll pass. Some people call me a picky eater. I prefer to think of myself as having discerning taste buds.

"I'm more of a strawberry jam kind of girl," I say.

"Well, I'm looking forward to sampling the local honey with my breakfast yogurt," she says.

I wonder if she knows that honey is basically a sort

of bee vomit. Bees chew and spit up nectar as part of the honey-making process. That's why I prefer strawberry jam. Just fruit and sugar mixed with a spoon. Simple and delicious. Deciding to keep my thoughts to myself, I ask them if they've ever visited Greece before.

She nods. "Many times. We love history and hiking, and Greece is the perfect place for both activities."

"And the food is to die for." Her husband rubs his stomach. "That's why we hike, so we can work off all the calories we consume."

"What about you?" the wife asks. "Is this your first time in Greece?"

"Uh-huh. My aunt rented a villa here for the summer."

"Well, you couldn't have picked a lovelier place to stay," she says. "Gáidaros is a beautiful island. This is our third time here."

"You have to try the spanakopita at Athena's while you're here," the husband says as he makes a chef's kiss. "Spinach and feta cheese in phyllo dough— delicious."

I really don't want to rain on his parade, but feta cheese smells like a teenage boy's sneakers. No, thank you. And don't even get me started on spinach. When it's raw, it makes your teeth feel weird, and in its cooked form, it turns sickly green and mushy and looks vile. I really hope they serve normal food on this island, like hamburgers and tacos.

"Since you're here for the whole summer, you'll be able to have spanakopita lots of times," the wife says.

"Oh, I'm only staying with my aunt for a couple of weeks. I can't afford to waste any more time than that."

She frowns. "Travel is never a waste of time. I wish I had done more traveling when I was your age."

"Actually, I travel all the time for my company. I meant that every day I'm on vacation means that I'm getting more and more behind with my work." I repress the urge to pull my phone out of my purse and check emails. Not that I could if I wanted to, since Maria cut off my access.

The man gives me a look that borders on pity. "You must work for an American company. Most of them only give their employees two weeks of vacation a year."

"My employer is actually quite generous with time off. It's just that there isn't enough time to take time off. . ." My voice trails off as I realize how ridiculous it sounds. Anxious to change the subject, I say, "It looks like we're docking."

As we collect our belongings, I overhear the man whisper to his wife, "She seems like one of those types who doesn't know how to have fun. I bet she works 24/7."

His wife hushes him, then gives me a wave as they disembark.

While I adjust the strap on my laptop case, I feel my face grow warm. So what if I like putting together spreadsheets and project plans on the weekends? That's my idea of fun. Spending two weeks twiddling my thumbs on a Greek island? I can't imagine anything less relaxing. But who knows, maybe something will happen to liven things up.

* * *

You should be careful what you wish for. As I'm getting off the ferry, the strap on my laptop bag breaks. I try to grab it, but it slips out of my hand. I watch in horror as the bag sinks into the water. One of the ferry workers fishes it out for me, but it's too late. There's no way this thing will work again.

Frank will be furious. He's always going on about how my department needs to keep expenses down. I can picture how he'll react when he learns my computer needs to be replaced. First, he'll give me the silent treatment, arms folded across his scrawny chest, his thin lips pressed together, and red, angry blotches forming on his pasty skin. Then the yelling will start. There will be relentless pacing back and forth while he tells me what an idiot I am.

"I expect you to put in extra hours to make up for wasting the department's budget," he'll say, knowing full well that I already work all hours of the day, not to mention burning the midnight oil on a regular basis. I'd be rich if I actually got paid for overtime.

It'll be easier if I just buy a new laptop using my own money rather than tell Frank what happened. I sigh as my laptop bag drips water on my shoes. Setting it down on a bench on the dock, I look around for Aunt Celeste. She was supposed to meet my ferry, but she's nowhere to be seen.

I perch on the bench and send her a text. After a few minutes, she replies.

Running late. Realigning my crystal aura taking longer than I thought. I'll be on the next ferry.

What in the world is a crystal aura? And why does it need to be realigned? And, wait a minute, what does she mean by the next ferry? She's not even on this island? Now, what am I supposed to do?

My stomach twists in knots as I survey my surroundings. The sun is beating down on me, reminding me that I forgot to pack a hat. The ferry workers are unloading crates, a fisherman is untangling a net, and a couple of goats tied up by a shed at the end of the dock are bleating.

I wipe sweat off my brow, wondering who I should approach for help. The ferry workers' English is limited and, based on the scowl on the fisherman's face, I doubt he'd welcome being interrupted. The goats seem like my best hope.

You're probably wondering why I need help. After all, I'm a seasoned international traveler, right? But here's the thing—I've never had to fend for myself.

Our team's administrative assistant books all my flights. Once I clear customs and immigration, someone is waiting there, holding a sign with my name on it. They whisk me away to my accommodations, where all my meals are provided. Then, I'm so busy with work that I never have a chance to explore my surroundings on my own. I'm basically taken care of, every step of the way.

Not this time, though. When Maria forced me to take vacation, my first thought was to spend two weeks holed up in my studio apartment in Minneapolis. But then my aunt convinced me that I should come visit her in Greece instead. "It'll be fun," she said.

So far, the fun has been non-existent. First, there was a ten-hour flight from Toronto to Athens crammed between a woman who couldn't stop talking about the sweaters she knits for her hamsters and a man wearing this pungent body spray that smelled like a cross between bubblegum and dog poop.

Next, I almost had a nervous breakdown trying to figure out how to get from the airport to the ferry terminal. That was followed by a sixteen-hour ferry ride to Rhodes. Fortunately, I slept for most of that leg of the journey. Unfortunately, when I woke up, I discovered that the cafe on board had run out of anything decent to eat.

But wait, there was more fun in store for me—another two-hour ferry ride from Rhodes to the nearby island of Gáidaros, my home for the next two weeks. If I can find my home, that is. Without Aunt Celeste here, I have no idea how to get to her villa.

As I look around frantically for help, my phone beeps.

Wait for me at Athena's, Aunt Celeste texts. *I should be there in a couple of hours.*

Athena's . . . That sounds familiar. Oh, yeah, it's the restaurant the Australian couple mentioned. I'm starved. A hamburger or a taco would hit the spot. I feel better. I have a plan. Now I just have to find where Athena's is located.

I gather my belongings. The ferry has departed, so I approach the fisherman. "Excuse me," I say. "Do you know where—"

Before I can finish my sentence, he starts his engine and pulls away from the dock.

"Thanks, buddy. You really know how to make tourists feel welcome," I say under my breath. Although why I'm speaking quietly is beyond me. The only ones left on the dock are me and the goats. The larger of the two bleats at me, probably telling me that I made a mistake coming to this island. Then he goes back to chewing on the rope that he's tied up to.

I watch him for a few minutes, impressed by the progress he's making. A few more bites and he'll be free.

"Is that tasty?" I ask.

The goat gives me side-eye as if to say, "Get lost,

lady. Go find your own food." He gives the rope one final chomp, then looks down at the frayed end lying on the dock as though perplexed by his freedom.

Who do you report goat escapees to? Do you call 911? Do they even have emergency services on this island? It's a pretty small place. I overheard someone on the ferry say that there are less than five hundred people living here.

The goat—who I'm now calling Houdini—ambles down the steps from the dock to the cobblestone path that presumably leads to the town. I glance down at Houdini's friend. He seems content to remain tied up, settling down on the ground next to the shed.

Houdini looks back at me and bleats insistently. You don't have to speak goat to know what he's saying. He's going to lead me to Athena's, I'm sure of it.

Of course, it could be delirium setting in rather than a sudden ability to understand goats. The sun is blazing hot, I'm weak from hunger, and I'm exhausted from my journey. But following a goat sure beats the alternative, which is waiting here until Aunt Celeste shows up on the next ferry.

"Okay, Houdini, let's go."

I trudge up the hill behind the goat, lugging my suitcase behind me. I'm grateful when he stops to chew on some grass on the side of the path. It gives me a chance to catch my breath. It really is beautiful here. Whitewashed buildings with blue roofs, colorful flowers spilling from planters, and a view of the Aegean Sea that is to die for.

Which reminds me, I might die soon if I don't get out of this sun and find something to eat.

"Houdini, can we get a move on?"

He looks at me blankly, then shrugs. At least I think it was a shrug. Do goats shrug? Never mind. What does it matter? We're moving again. The narrow path continues to wind up the hill, passing a church on our left before opening up onto a small plaza. The place is deserted. Where is everyone? Do they take siestas here?

I feel something tug at my skirt. It's the goat. "Hey, Houdini, find something else to eat," I say sharply.

He continues to tug at my skirt, pulling me toward a building at the far end of the plaza. Once there, he releases me, then wanders off to nibble on some flowers.

I run my fingers through my hair. "What do I do now?"

Houdini looks up from his snack and bleats loudly. I think what he's saying is, "I got you this far. Now, you're on your own."

Leaning against the building wall, I bang the back of my head against something. When I turn around to see what it is, I grin. A metal sign reads, "Athena's Taverna."

I say thank you to Houdini, then push open the rustic wooden door. An older woman wearing black from head-to-toe walks wearily toward me.

"Hi," I say brightly. "Are you serving lunch?"

She nods, then turns to get a menu. I check my phone and see that I've missed a text from my aunt.

Word of warning. Don't tell the lady who runs Athena's who you really are. If she asks about you, pretend you're Canadian. I'll explain later.

Um, okay. This is weird, even for my aunt. All I want is a simple hamburger or a taco, not to have to pretend to be from the Land of Maple Syrup. Don't get me wrong, I love maple syrup, but I'm a really bad actress. How in the world am I going to convince anyone that I'm Canadian?

CHAPTER 2
LOONIES AND TOONIES

As I put my phone back in my purse, my wallet falls out, strewing change all over the floor. The older woman helps me pick it up, then gives me a faint smile. "Why don't we seat you outside?" she suggests in English. Her long black skirt swishes behind her as she leads me past a table of guys wearing matching t-shirts emblazoned with their fraternity letters.

One of them grabs her arm as she walks by. "Hey Athena, can we get some more beer?" He lets out a loud belch, then adds, "Please."

She gives him an icy stare. "Don't you think y'all have had enough?"

I do a double take. Did this Greek woman, who looks like she's in mourning, just say "y'all" with a slight Texan drawl?

"Nah, we can hold our liquor," the frat boy says. One of his buddies holds his empty bottle in the air and chants, "Beer, beer, beer."

As the others join in, the chant turns to, "Athena, Athena, Athena."

"I wish I had never told them my name," she says to me. Then she looks back at the guys and says firmly, "I don't serve drunks."

One of them gives her an ingratiating smile. "How about if we recite the Greek alphabet? We wouldn't be able to do that if we had too much to drink, right?"

Athena accepts their challenge. "Agreed. But if you can't recite the entire alphabet, you leave. Okay?"

The frat boys get to their feet, slinging their arms around each other's shoulders to steady themselves. "Alpha, beta, gamma," they say together before coming to a halt.

"What comes after gamma?" one of them asks.

When no one can come up with the answer, Athena rolls her eyes. "I'll give you a hint. It's on your shirts." They stare at her blankly, and she adds, "The triangle-shape. What's it called?"

Their ringleader lets out another loud burp while the others look helplessly at each other.

"It's called delta," Athena says. "Are you sure you boys are in college? I know boxes of rocks brighter than you fellows."

They don't put up a fight when she ushers them out of the restaurant, probably because they're too busy blaming each other for being kicked out.

I shake my head. This is why I spent my time studying in college rather than going to parties. I was there to get a degree, not get drunk with a bunch of immature idiots. When I did date, I went for more serious guys whose idea of a good time was getting a pizza after studying in the library.

When Athena returns, she apologizes. "Sorry, you had to witness that. Americans can be so loud and obnoxious. Thankfully, it's usually only Australians and Canadians who visit our island. I think those boys boarded the wrong ferry and ended up here by mistake."

"But aren't you American?" I ask. "You sound like you're from Texas."

"I lived there for forty years," she says. "I can't seem to get rid of this ridiculous accent."

"I think your accent sounds cute."

"Cute?" She arches an eyebrow. "I'm a sixty-two-year-old widow. Cute isn't exactly what I'm going for."

I put a hand to my chest. "I'm so sorry. I didn't mean to offend you."

"That's what I like about you Canadians. You're always so polite."

"But I'm not—" Remembering Aunt Celeste's text, I stop myself. For some mysterious reason, she wants me to try to pass myself as someone from The Great White North. I smile at Athena and say, "So you think

I'm Canadian, eh?"

That "eh" was an inspired touch, I thought. The folks I worked with on the Toronto project were always saying it.

Athena gives me an appraising look. "Aren't you Canadian?"

"Yes, of course I am. I'm sorry," I blurt out. "I was just wondering what gave me away."

"Well, you have a soft accent, you apologize a lot, you said 'eh,' and you dropped all those loonies and toonies on the floor."

I furrow my brow. "Loonies and toonies?"

"Isn't that what you Canadians call your one-dollar and two-dollar coins?"

"Yes, you're right. Sorry about that. I don't know what I was thinking." Since I had flown directly from Toronto to Greece, the only money I had on me was Canadian. Turns out it was good camouflage.

"When's the last time you had something to eat?" Athena asks me. "You look pale."

"That's probably it," I say. "I'm hungry. It explains why I didn't remember what the Canadian, I mean, my country's coins are called."

The older woman leads me out onto a terrace which overlooks the harbor. After I sit down, she brings me some bottled water, then asks, "Are you traveling alone?"

I consider this for a moment. Technically, that's true. I came from Toronto to this island on my own, and I haven't met up with my aunt yet, so, yes, I'm traveling alone. When I say as much to Athena, she shakes her head. "A nice girl like you should have a boyfriend. Better yet, be married."

I nearly choke on my water. "Married?"

"Don't take this the wrong way," Athena says. "But when I was your age, I was already married with two kids."

How would a Canadian respond to this? Would they apologize for being nearly thirty and unmarried?

While I'm trying to figure out my response, Athena continues to chatter away, oblivious to my discomfort. "My son turned forty last week. He was one of those corporate types, working non-stop and too busy to settle down. Well, now that he's moved back to Gáidaros, he's going to get married to a nice Greek girl."

"Does he know that?" I ask dryly.

"He knows he's going to be married." She smiles. "What he doesn't know is *who* he's going to marry."

I lean forward. "Is this some sort of arranged marriage? Do you decide who he'll wed?"

"Don't be silly. He can decide what girl he marries as long as I approve of her." She looks down at the menu in front of me. "What would you like for lunch?"

"Could I get a hamburger?"

Athena narrows her eyes. "A hamburger?"

Why is she giving me that look? I've never been to

a place that doesn't have hamburgers. It's a universal kind of food. I like them because you know what you're getting—ground beef in a bun. Simple and straightforward. If I'm feeling daring, I'll have it with cheese, but only American or mild cheddar cheese. Nothing weird like blue cheese. Mold in my cheese? Yuck.

Pushing the menu toward me, Athena rattles off a list of dishes I've never heard of.

"Um, you don't happen to have any tacos, do you?"

Suddenly, Athena bursts out laughing. "Oh, I get it. You're pretending to be an American tourist. One of those types who stays at those all-inclusive Humpty Dumpty resorts where they serve all the hamburgers and tacos you can eat."

Then her tone grows more somber. "I heard a rumor that they're trying to open one of those resorts on a Greek island. Can you imagine? Mark my word, that will never happen here, not as long as I'm living."

I feel the blood draining from my face. It's bad enough that I've been pretending to be a Canadian. What would happen if Athena found out that I actually work for the Humpty Dumpty corporation? Feeling my muscles get tense, I take a deep breath and will myself to relax. It's going to be okay. I'm on vacation. No one needs to know what I do for a living or who I work for. There's no reason on earth why the subject will ever come up, right?

* * *

I stare out into the harbor, my stomach twisting in knots over my deception. Lying like this, pretending to be something I'm not—this isn't me. I could try to blame my people-pleasing personality, but that would be a cop-out. Sometimes, I think my whole life is one big cop-out.

Athena interrupts my thoughts, telling me she's going to bring me a Greek taco. My stomach rumbles at the thought of a taco, and I give her a big smile. When she comes back and sets a plate down in front of me, I furrow my brow.

"I'm sorry," I say. "Is this for me? It doesn't look like any taco I've ever seen."

"You're right, it's a gyros. But it's similar." Athena chuckles. "See, the pita bread is like a tortilla, and it's filled with meat and topped with cheese, tomatoes, and onions, just like a taco."

I poke at what is clearly *not* a taco with my fork. "Um, what kind of meat is it? And this white sauce on top, is that yogurt?"

"It's delicious, that's what it is. Now eat up, darlin'. You look like you're going to faint."

Fortunately, the gyros is served with a generous helping of fries. That's something I understand. I devour them. Then, when Athena is in the kitchen, I scrape the mystery meat and toppings off the pita bread and feed it to a dog who seems to have made himself at home on the terrace.

Athena returns and smiles when she sees my empty plate. "You were hungry. Can I get you anything else?"

I check the time on my phone. I have a while to wait for my aunt. "Coffee would be nice."

While I'm sipping on my third cup of coffee, I get another text.

Missed the ferry. I'll take the next one. Head up to the villa and I'll meet you there. Battery dying. Talk later.

I text Aunt Celeste back for directions, but she doesn't reply. I can't really ask Athena where the villa is because I have no idea what it's called or its general location. Sure, this is a small island, but getting directions to a vague unnamed villa that's located in some unspecified place is probably a stretch.

If I told Athena that I was looking for the villa being rented by a loud American woman named Celeste, that might help narrow things down. But my aunt was clear that I wasn't supposed to tell anyone who I really am, so that's out of the question. Why does she have me pretending to be a Canadian, anyway? I file that question away for later. Time to get moving and find this mystery villa.

I pay the bill and thank Athena for the delicious meal. Technically, that's not really a lie. I enjoyed the fries and the pita bread, and based on how quickly he devoured the gyros meat and toppings, the dog was satisfied with his food, too.

When I step back out onto the plaza, the shops are open and people are milling about. Siesta time must be over. I approach a group of men who are playing cards, intent on asking them directions. Then I realize the problem. I'm in the same boat as I was with Athena. Unless I tell them about Celeste, they're unlikely to know what villa I'm talking about. If I do tell them about Celeste, they might know where she's staying, but that also comes with a risk—it's a small island and word might get back to Athena that I'm not who I said I was.

The men look at me curiously. I give them a polite nod, then turn the other direction. A large fountain sits in the center of the plaza. Hot and sweaty from my long journey, I'm sorely tempted to plunge myself into the marble basin. Would a Canadian strip down and cool themselves off in the water? I'm not sure. It makes me realize there's so much I don't know about Canadians, despite the fact that I spent the past four months there. What do I really know about any of the countries I've worked in?

Before I can think too deeply about my cultural ignorance, Houdini ambles over and greets me with an enthusiastic bleat.

"You don't happen to know where my aunt's villa is, do you, little fellow?" I ask.

Houdini butts me with his head—which I take to mean "yes." Then he turns, obviously expecting me to follow him. So I do. He leads me to the opposite end of the plaza, then turns left onto a path leading further up the hill.

The path goes on for what seems like forever, one hairpin turn after another. Whenever we encounter anyone, they simply nod and smile. Foreigners with goats as their tour guides must be a common occurrence here.

Eventually, the path terminates in a small clearing surrounded by pine trees. In front of me is a brightly painted blue door set in the middle of a stone wall. A sign above the door reads "Villa Xenia." I spin around to ask Houdini if this is where Aunt Celeste is staying, but he's gone.

I spy a large brass bell and pull on the cord. After a few minutes without a response, I try again. No one is home, which makes me think this must be where my aunt is staying. Pushing open the door, I peer into the courtyard. "Hello, is anyone here?"

No one answers, so I tentatively walk inside. To my left is a classic Greek building—whitewashed walls, blue shutters, flowers spilling from window boxes, and balconies on the upper floors. To my right, a pergola covered with vines provides welcome shade over an outdoor kitchen and eating area. It's like something you'd see on an influencer's social media accounts.

In front of me is an infinity pool calling my name. Imagine soaking in the water, sipping on a cool drink while looking out at the Aegean Sea. I really hope this is my aunt's villa. Spending two weeks here might not be so bad after all.

A splashing noise startles me, and I realize I'm not alone. I watch as a man swims the length of the pool before surfacing in front of me. He lifts his head, shaking the water from his shoulder-length black hair before looking directly at me. His eyes are as dark as his hair. They're framed by thick lashes and are, frankly, pretty darn mesmerizing.

Wasn't there a Greek god who turned people into stone by mesmerizing them? Is that what's happening here? Is that why I have goosebumps? Are they a sign of an imminent transformation into a hard mass of mineral matter?

No, wait a minute, that wasn't a Greek god. It was a chick named Medusa. The one with snakes on her head instead of hair. Phew, I'm safe. I'm not going to be turned into stone. Regardless, I need to stop staring into this guy's eyes. I shift my gaze upwards. Good, eyebrows. Look at those. A totally non-sexual feature. Especially his. He's got a unibrow thing going on. If you asked me what physical features I find attractive in the opposite sex, an uninterrupted line of hair across a guy's forehead wouldn't make the list.

Mr. Unibrow interrupts my thoughts. "You must be Olivia. Celeste said you'd be arriving today."

"You know my aunt?"

Instead of answering, he hoists himself out of the pool. Water glistens on his dark olive skin. He's taller than me, but not so tall that I'd have to stand on my tiptoes to kiss him.

Kiss him? Where did that come from? It must be the fatigue. I don't go around thinking about kissing guys I've just met.

A faint smile plays across Mr. Unibrow's lips, almost as though he can read my mind. He walks over to a lounge chair and grabs a towel. As he dries himself off, I notice a tattoo on his right shoulder. Is that a taco tattoo?

Before I can be sure, he turns and faces me. "Celeste was right."

"Right about what?"

He wraps the towel around his waist, then says, "She's right about many things, don't you think?"

I press my lips together. I don't like the fact that Aunt Celeste has been talking to this guy about me. Not one bit. "Who exactly are you?"

"Xander," he says simply, as though that explains everything.

"Are you staying here at the villa?"

"Would you like me to?" he asks with a mischievous twinkle in his eye.

I want to say yes, which is ridiculous. Why would I want this unibrow guy to stay here? He's a complete stranger.

When I don't respond, he says, "Don't worry. I have my own place."

I put my hands on my hips. "If you're not a guest

here, why are you here?"

"Maybe I'm the pool boy," Xander says.

"Pool boys usually clean the pool. They don't swim in it. And when they're not cleaning the pool, they fetch towels and drinks."

"Ah, so that's the job description." Xander grabs another towel off the chair and tosses it at me. "Here you go. Now, I'll fetch you a drink."

He walks over to the outdoor kitchen. After a moment, I follow him, curious to see how this is going to play out. I perch on a barstool while he fills a tall glass with ice cubes. Next, he pours a cloudy white syrup into the glass before topping it off with some club soda.

"Have you ever had soumada before?" Xander asks as he pushes the drink toward me.

I eye the concoction warily. "No, what is it?"

"Why don't you try some and tell me what you think it's made of," he suggests playfully.

"Or you could tell me what's in it," I counter. "Then I might try it."

"Where's the fun in that?" He nods at the glass. "Go on, it won't bite."

Can you believe it? I take a sip. It's those eyes of his, I swear. They mesmerize you into doing stupid things like sampling mystery drinks. As the slightly sweet and slightly bitter liquid trickles down my throat, I smile. "That's delicious. Almonds?"

"Correct."

"I like almonds," I say before taking another sip.

"What is it that you like about almonds?" Xander leans forward, resting his elbows on the counter.

"I feel like you're about to analyze me."

"No, that would be way above my pay grade," he says. "Remember, I'm a pool boy. Towels and drinks. That's the limit of my powers."

"There's another flavor in there I can't put my finger on," I say.

"Ah, see, you're changing the subject. I asked you about almonds, remember?"

"Okay, fine. I like their shape."

He laughs. "That's a good enough reason as any."

"Your turn. What else is in this?"

"Orange peel, cloves, and cinnamon." Xander passes the syrup bottle to me. "It's a traditional drink on Crete."

I breathe a sigh of relief at the ingredient list. "Phew, those are all things I can eat."

"Yikes." His eyes widen. "I didn't realize you have food allergies."

"No, it's more like food preferences." I smile. "We have something in common. I like tacos, too."

He shakes his head. "I don't like tacos."

"But isn't that a taco tattoo on your shoulder?"

"Exactly."

"Do you always talk in riddles?"

"That wasn't a riddle. A riddle is when you say something, expecting the other person to figure it out."

"Believe me, I'm definitely trying to figure you out."

He shrugs. "Like I told you, I'm a simple pool boy. You've already got me figured out."

"How did a American pool boy end up in Greece?"

"American?" A smile plays across Xander's lips. "You've got the wrong guy."

Remembering how some of my colleagues in Toronto hated being mistaken for Americans, I apologize. "Sorry. You must be Canadian then."

"Nope. I'm from Gáidaros."

"But your English is so good."

"Well, don't tell anyone." He leans forward and lowers his voice. "I spent several years in Boston."

"Doing what?" I ask.

"Training to be a pool boy, of course. There's a lot to learn. How to fold towels, rub suntan lotion on women, and fetch drinks."

"Sun tan lotion rubbing. Hmm, sounds like an in-depth course."

"You have no idea," he says. "Some women are ticklish. What about you, Olivia? Are you ticklish?"

"No comment," I say.

"Don't worry, I'll ask Celeste."

"You and Celeste seem to be quite close," I say.

"She's a remarkable woman," he says. "I admire her determination to enjoy life and travel around the world, especially after the loss of her husband."

I nod. "She is pretty special."

As I reach for my soumada, a black cat jumps onto the counter and startles me. Xander grabs my glass before its contents spill out.

"That's Midnight," he says. "When I'm not around, he's the villa's caretaker."

"Ah, I knew it. You're not just a pool boy."

"Can't I be a caretaker and a pool boy?" he asks. "I'm a man of many talents."

"I'm sure you are," I say dryly.

He smiles in response, then turns to tidy up the outdoor kitchen.

"I suppose my aunt will be back soon," I say while absentmindedly stroking the cat.

"Didn't you know? The evening ferry from Rhodes was canceled. She won't be back until tomorrow." He places the syrup bottle on a shelf, then says, "Will you be okay here tonight on your own?"

"Of course. I'll have Midnight to keep me company."

Xander takes a piece of paper from a drawer and scrawls something down on it. "Here's my number. If you need anything, don't hesitate to call."

I shake my head. "I won't need anything."

"I wouldn't be so sure. You might get thirsty, need a new towel, or help applying suntan lotion on your back. That's when you need to call someone like me with the proper training and certifications to help."

Then Xander winks at me—a move which probably

doesn't have the effect he was hoping for because it draws attention to his unibrow—and takes his leave.

"I wish you could talk, Midnight," I say to the cat, "because I have a lot of questions. First of all, do you think my aunt has any normal food in the fridge for dinner? And second, what's the deal with Mr. Unibrow?"

CHAPTER 3
GOING UNDERCOVER

If I had a type, Xander would be the furthest thing from it. Sure, he's good looking—even that unibrow of his has a certain charm—but boy, is he ever secretive. Not one single straight answer to any of my questions.

Did you notice how he never said what he was doing at my aunt's villa? Just some gibberish about being a pool boy. And that nonsense about going to Boston to learn how to apply suntan lotion and fold towels? Please.

Okay, so maybe he really is the caretaker for the villa. But does that give him the right to swim in the pool? Caretakers don't use the facilities—they do cleaning and maintenance, that's it.

Xander acted like he and my aunt were joined at the hip. Did he somehow take advantage of my aunt's outgoing nature? She's gregarious, not to mention more than a tad eccentric. Aunt Celeste makes an impact the minute she walks into any room, befriending everyone who crosses her path. I'm sure she was nice to him, but that doesn't make them best buddies. Xander crossed the line for sure, swimming in the pool at the villa and acting like he owns the place.

In a way, he reminds me of those frat boys at the taverna—only interested in having a good time and not caring about how they affect others.

But you know what the kicker is? The man doesn't like tacos. Who in their right mind doesn't like tacos? Psychopaths, that's who. I'll talk with Aunt Celeste when she gets back tomorrow about getting this guy to back off.

I toss the paper with Xander's phone number into the trash. Then I carry my belongings inside the villa and locate my room. As I unpack my suitcase, a serious issue emerges, one that puts Xander completely out of my mind. I don't have a single thing to wear on this vacation.

My bag is full of business suits and pajamas. Other than what I'm currently wearing—a black linen skirt and a cream-colored sleeveless blouse—I don't have anything that could be even remotely described as casual wear. My life consists of going to work at the project site, grabbing a quick bite to eat, then going back to my room, changing into my pajamas and crashing for a few hours before doing it all over again. Because I flew directly from Toronto to Greece, I didn't have a chance to stop back at my apartment in Minneapolis and repack my suitcase with more suitable clothing.

I kick off my black flats, then slump onto the bed. This whole vacation thing is stressing me out. Not only am I going to be bored out of my mind for the next two weeks, now I have to go clothes shopping, something I hate.

Midnight pads into the room. He jumps up on the bed, sniffs at me curiously for a few moments before leaping into my partially unpacked suitcase. It's a good thing most of my suits are dark—the black fur he's shedding on them will blend right in.

I glance at my phone. It's already after six. Might as well change into my pajamas and call it a day. After donning my favorite PJs—the ones with a cute taco pattern on them—I head out to the patio area and make myself comfy on one of the lounge chairs. I pull up an ebook on my phone and try to focus on the cozy mystery I'm reading. Instead, all I can think about is Xander. That's the real mystery here—not who killed someone at a fictitious marina in Florida, but rather why this Greek guy keeps haunting my thoughts.

I must be hungry. Xander has a taco tattoo. Obviously, I'm craving a taco. That's the logical explanation, right? I shuffle off to the kitchen and rummage through the fridge and cupboards. As I'm trying to figure out what orzo is, my phone rings. I press it to my ear, expecting it to be my aunt.

"What did you do with the throughput analysis for the Dubai project?" a voice grumbles in my ear.

"Frank, is that you?" I'm so startled hearing my boss on the other end of the line that I drop the box of orzo. "Maria said that you're not supposed to call me. What if she finds out?"

"Please, you don't think I can outwit her? I'm calling you from a burner phone," Frank snaps. "Now, where's the spreadsheet?"

After explaining to him where I filed it on our shared server, I ask, "How is the project going? Were you able to find a replacement for me?"

"That's my girl," Frank says. "You're dedicated to the job. Vacations are wasted on people like you and me. We're nothing without work."

I start to protest, but then I realize he's right. It's not like I have any other hobbies or interests. Something gnaws at me, but I shake it off. Work fulfills me.

"Anyway, I wasn't sure if Her Highness Maria confiscated your laptop to keep you from doing any work," Frank says, his voice dripping with disdain. "So I went ahead and had another one couriered to you. It should be there sometime later tonight."

I breathe a sigh of relief. With a new computer on its way, I may get away without having to tell Frank about how my own laptop went for a swim in the harbor. "Does this mean you want me to work remotely on the Dubai project?"

"No, I have another assignment for you," Frank says. "A top secret one."

"You mean keeping it secret from Maria?" My stomach clenches at the thought of lying to her. Although she mandated this vacation because of company policy, I get the feeling that she also did it because she genuinely cares about my well-being. Whereas, Frank just cares about the bottom line.

"What Maria doesn't know won't hurt her," Frank says. "But this is bigger than keeping it secret from her. You need to keep this secret from everybody. We can't let our competitors get wind of this project."

I rush back into my room and grab a pad of paper and pen out of my bag. Frank doesn't like to repeat himself, so I need to be prepared to take notes. "What's the project? Where do I need to fly to?"

"You don't have to fly anywhere. You're already there." Frank chuckles. "Imagine my surprise when I found out the island you're slacking off on is the very same one where we're considering building a new Humpty Dumpty resort."

My jaw drops. "Here? On Gáidaros? How did you even know I'm staying here?"

"You don't think I know how to keep tabs on my employees? I know where you are every minute of the day."

Um, well, that's a bit worrying. I'm not sure I like

the idea of my boss monitoring my movements, but I decide to keep that to myself. "Why Gáidaros?" I ask.

"It's the perfect site. Small picturesque island away from the hustle and bustle of it all. Our guests can relax in style in luxury bungalows overlooking the Aegean Sea and enjoy the ultimate all-inclusive Humpty Dumpty experience. You know what we say. It's like..."

"It's like being back home in the States, but better," I chime in.

"That's right," Frank says. "Our guests like to visit exotic locations, but with all the American comforts they're used to. Our strategy team thinks Gáidaros might be just the ticket. Of course, we're still in the feasibility assessment stage. That's where you come in."

"What do you need me to do?" I ask, my pen poised to scribble down my instructions.

"It's pretty straightforward. We need you to visit potential building sites, take photos, and gather information and data. I'll send you the details in an email."

My shoulders tense. "An email? Maria is monitoring my company account."

"Do I have to spell everything out for you, Olivia?" Frank barks into the phone. "You have a personal email account, don't you? I'll contact you there."

After I give Frank my email address, he says, "You're staying with your grandmother, right?"

"It's my aunt," I say.

"Grandmother, aunt, whatever," Frank says impatiently. "Just don't tell the old broad about what you're working on. Don't tell anyone. This is top secret. Got it?"

After Frank hangs up, I review my notes. Part of me is excited. Working on a project like this is a big step on the career ladder. But the other part of me feels sick about being an undercover spy for the company. I'm going to have to lie to my aunt. I'm not sure I can be convincing. She's always had a way of seeing through me.

A voice calls out, interrupting my thoughts. "Olivia, are you there?"

It's a man's voice, one I'm pretty sure belongs to Xander. I tuck my notes into my bag, then check my hair in the mirror. My bob is looking more tousled than normal. I smooth it down, then walk out into the living room.

"There you are," Xander says. He's dressed casually in a white linen shirt, khaki pants, and leather sandals. Motioning at a large cardboard box on the coffee table, he says, "This came for you on a speedboat from Rhodes. Must be urgent. Most packages usually arrive on the ferry."

I arch an eyebrow. "So, in addition to being a pool boy, you're also a delivery boy?"

"I was at the harbor when it came," he says with a shrug. "I offered to bring it up to you since I was already coming this way."

"Didn't you get enough swimming in for one day already?"

"I'm not here to swim, although we can go skinny dipping later if you'd like."

My eyes widen. "Skinny dipping?"

He chuckles at my discomfort. "Don't worry. I was kidding."

Based on the tone of his voice and the way he's looking at me, I'm not entirely sure that's true. "What are you really doing here?" I say abruptly.

"Celeste called me. She was worried that you wouldn't have anything to eat. Apparently, you're not a great cook."

"I'll have you know that I make a mean grilled cheese."

"How very gourmet of you," he says with a smirk. "However, I think we can do better than that."

"Don't worry, I'll be fine." I pick up the cardboard box and walk toward the door, hoping he'll take the hint. "Thanks for the delivery."

"That's not all I brought," he says behind me. "Celeste made me promise that I'd feed you dinner."

"She did what?" I spin around and see Xander holding up a picnic basket.

"Shall we eat outside?" he asks as he brushes past me. "It's a nice night."

Apparently, I don't have any fight left in me because I follow him out to the patio, still clutching the cardboard box in my arms.

As Xander sets the basket down on the patio table, he eyes my box. "What's inside?"

"It's a laptop for my new work project," I say.

"Work? I thought you were on vacation?"

My face burns. It's been only a few minutes since Frank gave me my assignment and I've already slipped up. I'm not exactly cut out as an undercover corporate spy. Crossing my fingers behind my back, I say, "Yep, vacation. That's me. Rest and relaxation 24/7."

He grins. "Based on the way you're dressed, I'd say you have that nailed."

"What do you mean . . ." My voice trails off as I realize what Xander was talking about. I'm wearing pajamas. Taco pajamas at that. Well, this is embarrassing. Not that I care what he thinks about how I look. Not one bit.

* * *

While Xander unpacks the picnic basket, I take my box to my room. After I open it, Midnight comes over to investigate. He's thrilled that there's something new to sit in, promptly shedding fur all over my new laptop before I can get it out of the box.

While the cat settles down for a nap, I debate whether or not to change clothes. But what would I wear? The skirt and blouse I had on earlier today are dusty and dirty. My only other option is a suit. Uh, yeah, that would be kind of ridiculous.

I glance down at the pajamas I'm wearing. These will have to do. They're loose and comfortable, and they bring out the blue in my eyes. Not that I care if Xander notices what color my eyes are. He has dark eyes. I have light eyes. I love tacos. He hates them. I'm a professional. He's completely unprofessional. Opposites in every way. And, despite what they tell you, the whole "opposites attract" thing is a bunch of nonsense. Who wants to be with someone they have nothing in common with? Not me, that's for sure.

When I return to the patio, Xander is putting the finishing touches on the table setting. Blue and white patterned plates, rustic wine glasses and flickering candles sit on top of a woven tablecloth. The ambiance is more suited for a romantic date, not dinner for a girl wearing taco pajamas and a pool boy with a unibrow.

"Was that your stomach growling?" Xander looks up at me and smirks. "Someone sure is hungry."

I am hungry, but not for the food he has laid out—dark green blobs in a casserole dish, a bowl of beige goo, and a plate of what looks like fried tentacles. I look around for the cameras. Surely, this is one of those reality shows where the people eat food straight out of a horror movie in the hopes of winning large cash prizes and bragging rights.

Xander clears his throat. He's pulled out a chair for

me and is waiting for me to sit.

"Sorry," I say. "It's just so, um, overwhelming."

"I hope you like dolmades," he says.

I place my napkin on my lap, then ask, "Which one is that? The blobs or the goo?"

"Blobs and goo." Xander has a bemused look on his face. "That's the first time anyone has described my cooking that way."

"You made this?"

"Well, not the pita bread." He removes a piece of cloth which is covering a basket. "I got that from the bakery."

I do a fist pump when he unveils the Greek pita bread. Finally, something I can eat. I place a piece on my plate, then say, "So, in addition to being a pool boy and a delivery boy, you're also a cook."

Xander places a couple of green blobs on my plate, then informs me he prefers the term "chef."

"'Chef' is usually reserved for someone who's received formal training and works in a restaurant or a hotel," I say.

"I stand corrected," he says dryly.

I eye the blobs on my plate warily before poking them with a fork.

Xander chuckles. "They won't bite."

I'm still dubious. "Are these leaves?"

"Yes, but not just any leaves. They're grape leaves which are stuffed with rice and minced meat."

"Leaves stuffed with food. Interesting concept." I

set my fork down, then tear off a piece of my pita bread.

"Why don't you try some melitzanoalata with that?" When I give him a blank look, he smiles. "That's the goo, as you so charmingly call it."

"Oh, is that salad?" I point at a bowl on the opposite side of the table.

Xander blocks my efforts to grab the bowl. "You can have salad after you try some of the blobs and goo."

My stomach gurgles again, reminding me how hungry I am. Although the pita bread is delicious, I'm not sure it's going to fill me up. I might just have to force down some of Xander's concoctions.

"Fine," I grumble.

Xander spreads some of the goo onto a piece of bread, then hands it to me. "Melitzanoalata is made out of eggplant. I charred it on the grill, then added garlic, olive oil, lemon juice, and herbs."

After taking a cautious bite, I say, "I don't hate it."

Xander rolls his eyes. "I'll take that as a compliment. Now try the dolmades."

I'm not sure I can do this. The only green things I eat are lettuce, M&M's, and lime Jell-O. Spinach, peas, green beans, and grape leaves are most certainly not on my list of approved foods. "Maybe I'll just have more of the meli . . . How do you say that again?"

"Melitzanoalata."

After trying to repeat what he's said a few times, I

shake my head. "That's too hard. Let's stick to calling it goo."

Xander gets up from the table and walks behind my chair. I startle as he places his hands on my shoulders. "Close your eyes," he whispers in my ear, sending shivers down my spine.

"Why would I do that?" I'm embarrassed at how shaky my voice sounds. Pulling away slightly, I twist my head and look at Xander. His face is hidden in the shadows, making his expression hard to read.

"What are you scared of, Olivia?" His tone is light, but there's an undercurrent of something else. Something that makes me nervous.

"I don't know what you're talking about." This time my voice sounds normal, or at least I hope it does.

"Prove it. Close your eyes and try some of the dolmades. Focus on what it tastes like, not what it looks like."

Squeezing my eyes shut, I say, "Bring it on."

Xander chuckles as he feeds me some of the blobs. Between you and me, it's not bad, but there's no way I'm going to tell him that.

"Well, what did you think?" Xander asks as he returns to his seat.

"I'll stick to the goo and salad, if you don't mind." I point at the plate of fried tentacles. "Don't even think of putting any of those on my plate."

Xander looks crestfallen, and now I feel guilty. He

did go to the trouble of making this meal himself. But before I can apologize, he leans forward and says, "Did I mention that we're going to the archaeological ruins on the west side of the island tomorrow?"

I fold my arms across my chest. "You know I'm perfectly capable of making my own plans."

"I'm sure you are. Sounds like it will just be me and Celeste." He gives me a cocky grin, then asks, "So, what are your plans tomorrow?"

"Well, I'm, uh . . ." Oh, crap. I just remembered one of the things Frank wants me to do tomorrow, namely check out the archaeological ruins to see if it would be a suitable building site. I plaster a smile on my face. "You know what? An expedition with you and Celeste sounds fun. Count me in."

CHAPTER 4
TACO PAJAMAS

When I wake up the next morning, I can already tell it's going to be a bad day. I barely slept a wink last night. Indigestion from the strange food Xander made me eat, and Frank's constant texts about the Gáidaros feasibility study kept me tossing and turning.

As I get ready, thoughts about Frank and Xander fill my mind. The Frank stuff is pretty straightforward —how to keep on top of the task list he's given me. When it comes to Xander, that's way more complicated.

After dinner was over, I told Xander to leave the dishes and that I would clean up. He tried to help, but my repeated yawns convinced him that I really was exhausted from my travels. Before leaving, he kissed me on both cheeks in a casual European way.

I felt a sudden rush of warmth through my body as the stubble on his chin lightly scratched my skin. Fighting the urge to turn my face so that his lips would brush against mine was hard. Can you imagine if I had given into that temptation? What would Xander have done if our lips touched? Would he have looked shocked and pulled away? Or would he have kissed me back?

See what I mean—thinking about Xander is complicated. And the last thing I need in my life is complications. I'm here on Gáidaros for work, not to fall for a Greek pool boy.

As I blow dry my hair, I wonder if things would be different if Frank hadn't called. If I was truly on vacation, would I allow myself to get involved with Xander? Is a short-term romance something I would want?

I set the hairdryer down on the bathroom vanity and look at myself in the mirror. I straighten my shoulders, smile brightly at myself, and try to project an air of confidence. *You're here on business,* I tell myself. *Stop acting like a lovesick teenager.*

My fake smile turns into a genuine one when I hear Aunt Celeste call out, "Olivia, dear, where are you?"

I rush into the hallway, excited to see her. As my aunt pulls me into a warm embrace, she asks, "How long has it been since I last saw you?"

"It was at Shane and Audra's wedding," I say.

"Your cousin Shane got married three years ago."

Aunt Celeste wags a finger at me. "That's too long not to see my favorite niece."

I snort. "I'm your only niece."

"True. Boys do seem to run in the family." She kisses me on the cheek. "But I still would like to see you more often. You need to stop working so hard."

"You've been talking to my mom, haven't you?"

"She's thrilled that you're finally taking a vacation."

"It's a shame she and my dad had already booked a cruise. But when they heard what a great time you had on your transatlantic voyage from Florida to Italy, they immediately snagged a last-minute deal," I say. "I can't blame them, but I would have liked to have seen them."

"Well, you're stuck with me," she teases. "Now, you better get changed. Xander is going to be here at ten to take us to the archaeological ruins. You wouldn't want him to see you in those taco pajamas, would you?"

"He's already seen me in them," I say.

Aunt Celeste's jaw drops. "He has?"

My face grows warm as I realize what she's thinking. "No, not like that. I just met him yesterday. I wouldn't—" I splutter.

"Sorry. I didn't mean to embarrass you. Who you date is none of my business."

I burst out laughing. "None of your business? Please. You're always getting involved in people's love lives. Shane would have never asked out Audra if it hadn't been for you."

"Guilty as charged." She grins as she holds her hand to her chest. "Now, spill. Tell me all about you and Xander. He's a wonderful young man. The first time I met him, I knew the two of you would hit it off."

"There isn't anything to tell. I was in my pajamas when Xander brought dinner over last night. End of story."

"Or maybe it's the start of the story." She gives me a mischievous smile, then grabs her suitcase. "I'm going to freshen up before your Romeo gets here."

I roll my eyes, then head back to my room to change. But change into what? The clothes I was wearing yesterday need to be washed and my pajamas are out of the question. That leaves me with my business wear. I grab the pants from my navy pinstripe suit and pair them with a pale pink silk blouse. I leave the bow on the blouse untied to give it a more casual look. Then I slip my white Converse sneakers on and call it good.

When I join my aunt on the patio, she raises her eyebrows at my outfit, but doesn't say anything. She's dressed more appropriately for touring an archaeological site—khaki capri pants and a short-sleeved cotton top.

I hear a loud grating noise outside the courtyard wall. "What was that?"

Aunt Celeste claps her hands together. "I think our ride is here."

"That car sounds like it needs some new belts."

My aunt cocks her head to one side. "There aren't any cars on the island."

I get flashbacks to an ill-fated childhood trip to the zoo and it dawns on me what that noise is. As I walk toward the gate, I say, "Oh, please tell me you're kidding."

When I fling the gate open, Xander is standing on the other side. I barely give him a glance. Well, technically, that's not true. I eye him from head to toe, taking in his jeans, t-shirt, dark eyes, cocky smile, and unibrow. But it's the three shaggy creatures next to him that I'm really focusing on.

I put my head in my hands. "Why did it have to be donkeys? I hate donkeys."

* * *

My last donkey encounter was when I was seven years old. Do you have any idea how embarrassing it is to have a donkey pull down your pants in front of the rest of the class? What made it worse was that I was wearing my Wonder Woman underwear.

Before that day, I thought Wonder Woman was the best. A female superhero who was strong, assertive, and could kick butt? Yes, please! I aspired to be Wonder Woman when I grew up. I could picture myself wearing a red, white and blue superhero costume and brandishing a lariat at bad guys.

Until then, donning that pair of underwear in elementary school made me feel invincible. With them on, I'd be able to solve math problems with ease and stand up to bullies on the playground.

But, after being laughed at by the other students, I renounced that lariat-wielding superhero. Barbie became my role model instead. A stunning girl with gorgeous clothes and an impossible to obtain figure? Why not? Insecurity has to start somewhere.

I had hoped to never encounter another donkey again in my lifetime. Now here I am, facing three of them. The two standing to Xander's left are gray and surly looking. Fortunately, they're silent. That's the most positive thing I can say about them.

The donkey to the right of Xander has brown and white patches and can't shut up. It continues to bray until Xander pulls a carrot out of a bag. Finally, some peace and quiet while the obnoxious creature consumes his treat.

While Xander strokes the donkey's neck and speaks to it in Greek, Aunt Celeste tugs at my elbow. "Are you okay, Olivia?"

"I was fine until Larry, Curly, and Mo showed up."

Xander shoots me a look. "Are you comparing my donkeys to the Three Stooges?"

"No, you're right. That's not fair," I say. "The Three Stooges were far more good looking than these guys. Smarter too."

"Donkeys are exceptionally intelligent." Xander hands out a few more carrots, then adds, "Their problem-solving ability is phenomenal. I'd say it's on par with that of dolphins."

"So, in addition to being a pool boy, you're also a zoologist?" I ask.

"What can I say? I'm a man of many talents." Xander purses his lips. "What about you, Olivia? What are your talents? You never told me what you do for a living."

I ignore his question, instead firing back, "Why do they have saddles?"

"If you'd prefer to ride bareback to the archaeological site, we can arrange that."

The way Xander says that sounds almost like a dare, but there's no way I'm taking that bait.

"Tell you what, how about if we leave Larry, Curly, and Mo here and drive to the site instead?"

Xander's eyes crinkle with amusement. "Oh, I see what's going on. You have a form of equinophobia."

"I'm not afraid of donkeys." Folding my arms across my chest, I add, "I just don't like them."

Aunt Celeste looks back and forth at the two of us and chuckles. "Well, I see the two of you certainly hit it off in my absence."

I shake my head. It's been less than twenty-four hours since I first laid eyes on Xander. In that short space of time, he's jumbled up my emotions so much that I hardly know what I'm feeling right now. Irritation for sure, but also something else that I can't quite describe. Or maybe I don't want to describe it because that would make it real.

"Honey, there aren't any vehicles on the island," my aunt reminds me. "People use donkeys to get around."

I point at my Converse sneakers. "We have feet. We can use them to get there."

Xander shrugs. "It's around fifteen kilometers there and back. Celeste is going to ride one of the Three Stooges, but feel free to walk if you'd like."

While I'm mentally calculating how many miles that is, my aunt says, "There's no way you can walk that far. Given how you feel about donkeys, why don't we skip the trip and relax by the pool instead today?"

Before I can reply, my phone rings. "Hang on a minute. I need to answer this." I retreat back into the house to take the call in private.

"Where's my site assessment report?" Frank barks.

"It's only ten in the morning," I say nervously. Frank is known for setting impossible deadlines and then raging when they're not met.

"What does that have to do with anything?"

"We're heading out to the archaeological site now. When I get back, I'll write up the report."

"We?" Frank asks harshly. "I told you that this project was confidential. You're not supposed to tell anyone about it."

"I haven't," I say quickly. "My aunt had arranged for us to go visit the site before you told me about it. But I swear, she doesn't know about my real reason for going there."

He considers this for a moment, then says. "Okay. I guess an old lady won't be an issue. Just make sure no one else is involved."

"Well, about that," I say slowly. "There's the donkey guy."

"Donkey guy?"

"We have to ride donkeys to get to the site. They're his donkeys."

"Fine. I suppose some Greek peasant won't be an issue." My boss lets out an exasperated sigh. "Do you think you can handle another assignment, or is that too much for your delicate nature so early in the morning?"

I don't bat an eye at Frank's sarcasm. I'm used to it. For some reason, he thinks it's an effective management technique. "Of course. What's the assignment?"

"There's a major landowner on the island who I need you to cozy up to. He owns some rental properties, a lot of acreage, and other prime real estate. Make an excuse to meet him and ingratiate yourself. I need you to schmooze him so that when we're ready to start negotiations, he'll be putty in your hands." Frank pauses to yell instructions to his secretary, then adds, "Remember, don't tell him about the project."

I gulp. "You mean I have to lie to him?"

"Do you want to get ahead or not, Olivia? Lying is part of how business is done. If you can't get on board, I need to know now." When I don't answer right away, Frank's tone softens ever so slightly. "The guy is going to become rich as a result of this deal. You'll be doing him a favor."

"What's his name?" I say softly.

"Alexander Papadakis."

"Okay. I'll see if I can find out who he is."

"There are less than five hundred people on the island," Frank snaps. "How hard can it be?"

After giving me a few more directives, Frank hangs up. When I rejoin Aunt Celeste and Xander outside, I gesture at the Three Stooges. "Which one of these is mine?"

Xander points at the noisy brown and white donkey. "There you go, Homer Papadakis, at your service."

"You don't mind if I call him Curly, do you? Remember how Curly would say, 'nyuk-nyuk-nyuk' in a high-pitched voice? I bet if you closed your eyes and listened to Homer bray, it would sound exactly the same."

"His name is Homer Papadakis," Xander repeats.

I wave a hand in the air. "Homer, I can deal with. But the rest is too hard for me to pronounce. Besides, it sounds like a pizza place."

"Olivia, you're being rude," my aunt says to me. "Don't make fun of Xander's last name."

"Wait a minute, your last name is . . ." My voice trails off as I put two and two together.

"Papadakis," Xander says impatiently.

I take a deep breath. "Is Xander short for Alexander, by any chance?"

He makes a mocking bow. "Alexander Papadakis, at your service."

Well, this should make Frank happy. Turns out the donkey boy is also the major landowner I'm supposed to cozy up to.

CHAPTER 5
HATE-FLIRTING

I'm thrilled when Aunt Celeste suggests we walk to the plaza and get some coffee before heading to the archaeological site. Caffeine and delaying this stupid donkey ride is a win in my books. Xander leads the donkeys behind us. I glance back periodically to make sure they keep their distance. I don't want a repeat of my childhood pants-pulling incident. At least, I'm not wearing Wonder Woman underwear this time, but still.

As we make our way to the plaza, Aunt Celeste tells me about traditional Greek dancing. "The kalamatianós is my favorite. Everyone holds hands and dances in a circle. Have you seen *My Big Fat Greek Wedding*? They perform the kalamatianós at the end."

"I've heard of it, but I've never seen it," I say.

"We have to watch it while you're here. It's such a cute movie." My aunt glances back at Xander, then lowers her voice. "It's about a Greek-American woman who falls for a non-Greek guy. Sound familiar?"

I know what Aunt Celeste is driving at, but I don't want to encourage her. "Not even remotely."

My aunt loops her hand through my arm and draws me closer. "Her family doesn't approve. But true love prevails in the end, as it always does."

"What are you two whispering about?" Xander calls out.

"I'm just telling Olivia about how much I love dancing," my aunt says.

While they chat about the traditional costumes that Greek dancers wear, my mind drifts off. I can't stop thinking about the fact that Xander the pool boy would turn out to be Alexander Papadakis, a major landowner on Gáidaros. Why does Xander have to be the same guy Frank wants me to cozy up to? What does "cozy up to" even mean? Are we supposed to snuggle under a blanket and drink cocoa?

Frank is delusional if he thinks Xander is going to sell his land without a fuss and let his island be turned into a Humpty Dumpty resort. Last night, while we were having our dinner of goo and blobs, Xander talked about how much he loves Gáidaros and its traditional, quiet way of life. Once he finds out about it, Xander will resist Humpty Dumpty's plan with every fiber of his being. I need to find a way to convince Frank that this resort development isn't going to work.

"You're going to love this 'kafeneio,'" Aunt Celeste says, interrupting my thoughts. "That's what you call a coffee shop in Greek. You should learn a few phrases while you're here. It'll help you fit in better."

Sure. I should learn how to say "corporate spy," "hostile takeover," and "backstabber" in Greek. That'll come in handy if Xander finds out who I really am.

I mentally shake myself. It doesn't do any good to dwell on "what ifs." There's no reason Xander will ever find out. By the time any announcement comes out about the resort, I'll be long gone.

Turning my thoughts to more important things like coffee, I snap a picture of the kafeneio with my phone. It looks like something out of a travel magazine. Wooden tables and chairs painted in various shades of blue are situated on either side of the entrance, terracotta planters overflowing with red and orange flowers add a punch of color against the whitewashed walls, and a rooster crows nearby.

While Xander ties the donkeys up to a nearby tree, my aunt takes a seat at one of the tables. "What exactly happened last night between you two?" she asks me in a hushed voice.

"What do you mean?"

She gives me a knowing look. "You know exactly

what I mean. You've been hate-flirting with Xander all morning."

I hold up my hands. "There's no flirting of any kind going on here."

"Oh, the lies we tell ourselves."

When Xander walks back toward us, I make a "zip it" motion at my aunt.

"You should come in and see how the coffee is made," Xander says to me. "It's a fascinating process."

"Sure," I say. Anything to get him away from my aunt before she says something else about Xander and me. Not that there's a "Xander and me." There's just Xander and there's me. Completely separate entities.

Inside, the owner smiles at me before greeting Xander. While they're chatting, I look out the window, secretly hoping I'll catch a glimpse of my friend, Houdini the goat. Instead, I see Athena marching across the plaza toward the kafeneio. She comes to a halt in front of my aunt, narrows her eyes, then spits three times on the ground.

"What's wrong?" Xander asks when he hears me gasp.

"Do you know that lady?" I point at Athena. "She just spit at my aunt. Seriously, who does that?"

"I wouldn't take it too seriously. She's just upset," Xander says.

"I don't understand why. Everyone loves my aunt." When Athena purses her lips as though she's going to spit again, I say, "I need to put a stop to this."

Before I can storm out to rescue my aunt, Xander pulls me back. "I wouldn't get involved if I were you. Your aunt can fight her own battles."

"Athena looks like she can hold her own, too," I say.

"She's had a lot of practice," Xander says with a wry smile.

I'm not sure what to make of his response, but before I can ask him to elaborate, Xander guides me back to the counter to see how our coffee is prepared.

We watch as the owner of the kafeneio brings water up to a boil in a copper pot, then adds some finely ground coffee, stirring it briefly. Each time the coffee foams, he takes it briefly off the heat until it settles, then places it back on the heat. After doing this several times, he pours the coffee into blue demitasse cups, then says something to Xander in Greek.

"He wants to know how much sugar you want," Xander explains. "I told him you're a 'variglykos' kind of girl."

"I hope that means I take my coffee black."

Xander shakes his head. "Trust me. You need sugar, otherwise it would be too strong and bitter for you."

"I can handle strong and bitter."

"I'm sure you can," Xander grins. "Sketos it is."

Athena is gone by the time Xander and I rejoin my aunt outside. She smiles at the two of us, then asks

Xander if he wouldn't mind getting her some cookies. "I can't remember what they're called. The twisted ones you dip in coffee."

"Koulourakia?" Xander asks as he sets her cup down.

"Yes, those are the ones."

While Xander is inside, I put my hand on my aunt's arm. "Why did Athena spit at you?"

"Honestly, I don't know." My aunt frowns. "But she's had it in for me from the first day we met."

"There has to be a reason why she hates you so much." I arch an eyebrow. "You're keeping something from me."

"You're making a mountain out of a molehill," Aunt Celeste says before taking a sip of her coffee.

"I feel like there's more going on here than meets the eye." I look around to make sure no one can overhear me. "Why in the world did you have me pretend to be a Canadian when I went into Athena's taverna?"

"I didn't think you'd be able to pull off an Italian accent."

"Well, that's probably true. But why did I have to fake being something I'm not?"

"You saw how she spit at me. I didn't want her taking out whatever she has against me on you." My aunt shushes me. "Xander's coming. We'll talk more about this later."

As Xander sets the plate of cookies down in front

of us, he asks if I like my coffee. "Not too strong and bitter?"

I take a sip from my cup and fight back a grimace. Man, this stuff could use some sugar, but there's no way I'm telling Xander that. I give him a big smile. "It's great."

Xander locks his eyes with mine for a beat, as if trying to tell if I'm lying. I don't flinch under his scrutiny. Then he turns to my aunt. "I was thinking that the three of us should have dinner at the taverna tomorrow tonight. Spanakopita is on the menu. I remember how much you enjoyed it last time."

While my aunt nods enthusiastically, I butt in. "There's two problems with your plan. First is the fact that Athena just spat at my aunt. If that's how she behaves in a public place, imagine what she would do if my aunt tried to walk into her taverna?"

"You're right. That could be quite the scene." Xander chuckles. "But it would also give the town something new to gossip about."

Aunt Celeste squeezes my hand. "Don't worry. It will be fine. It's about time she and I cleared the air, anyway."

"See, problem solved," Xander says.

I hold up my hand. "Don't forget, there's another problem with your plan. Spanakopita is made with spinach, right? I'm not a big fan of green mush."

* * *

While Xander and my aunt dawdle over their coffee and cookies, my anxiety ratchets up. It's after eleven. We need to get a move on and see these archaeological ruins. Frank is expecting his report. And believe me, you don't want to miss one of Frank's deadlines.

When I start drumming my fingers on the table, they finally take the hint.

After getting my aunt situated on her donkey—whose name is Marge for some reason—Xander turns to me. "Do you need help getting in the saddle?"

I press my lips together. "No. Just hold Curly still."

"His name is Homer," Xander reminds me.

"Whatever. It's not like I'm going to be sending him Christmas cards." When Homer lets out an indignant bray, I wag a finger at him. "You're a donkey. You can't read Christmas cards, anyway."

"He might appreciate the picture on the front," Xander says. "He's partial to snowmen."

"How discerning of him," I mutter as I step into the stirrup.

Xander seems surprised at how smoothly I get into the saddle. "I thought you hated donkeys."

I narrow my eyes. "It's more like donkeys hate me."

"Homer doesn't have a mean bone in his body," Xander informs me. He glances over at my aunt, checks to make sure she's okay, then tells us to follow him.

"Why aren't you riding your donkey?" I call out as Xander leads us out of the plaza.

He turns and grins. "His name is Bart."

"Okay, why aren't you riding Bart?"

"I weigh more than you and your aunt." Xander taps the leather saddle bags strapped on Bart's back. "It would be too much for him to carry me and our supplies."

"You're going to walk the entire way?"

He shrugs. "I'm used to walking long distances."

When I try to dismount, Aunt Celeste intervenes. "Half the fun is the donkey ride. Besides, it's a steep climb up the hill. You don't want to walk that."

Not wanting to disagree with my aunt, I stick with Homer. A decision I soon regret. He's got a pretty unpleasant odor to him. Do they make body spray for donkeys? If they do, this guy sure needs some. And his gait is slow and plodding. If Homer was racing a turtle, the turtle would win by a mile.

Homer and I quickly fall behind the others, and I resign myself to a long, smelly donkey ride. My thoughts drift off, alternating between stressing out about Frank's report and wondering about Xander's tattoo. If he hates tacos so much, why did he get a tattoo of one?

There's so much I want to know about this guy. For starters, why was he pretending to be a pool boy? Okay, maybe he was just joking about it, but why hide the fact that he owns huge chunks of land on this island?

Wait a minute, is Xander rich? That's something I hadn't considered before, not that that sort of thing matters to me. I like smart, serious guys who are self-effacing and work hard in their chosen profession. What they do and how much money they make doesn't matter. In fact, based on my last boyfriend, I'd say guys who are laser focused on making a buck tend to see women as arm candy, not as an equal partner.

Homer comes to an abrupt stop, jolting me back to reality. In a way, I was thankful to the donkey because I didn't like the way my mind was thinking about Xander in terms of whether or not he'd make a good boyfriend.

Xander turns and looks back at me. "Stop dawdling. Celeste is way ahead of us."

"Can I help it if my donkey is a dud?" I ask. "He stops every five minutes to eat whatever is growing on the side of the path. Grass, flowers, weeds—doesn't matter. He'll snarf it down."

"I'm not sure that's Homer's fault." Xander smirks. "It might have something to do with his rider."

I press my lips together. "I'll have you know that I've been riding horses since I was a girl."

"Well, there's your problem," he says. "Homer is a donkey, not a horse."

"Same thing, more or less," I say.

"That's like saying ice cream and soft serve are the

same thing."

"Well, they are."

"Far from it." Xander leads his donkey over toward me. "Soft serve tries to imitate ice cream, but it's a poor substitute full of air and chemicals."

"I like soft serve."

"Why doesn't that surprise me? You have the taste buds of a five-year-old."

"Do not."

"Do too."

"Now, who's acting like a child?" I wrinkle my nose. "Did you smell that? Homer just farted."

Xander takes a step back. "Maybe that's because he can sense that you have no respect for his species."

"The only thing Homer can sense is food. And that's even a stretch. I swear he ate a rock earlier, which could explain why he's stinking up the place." I pinch my nose until the air clears. "The original Homer was one of the greatest authors of all time. I'm not sure this guy is bright enough to be named after someone who wrote the *Iliad* and *Odyssey*."

Xander chuckles. "He's actually named after Homer Simpson."

"The cartoon character? That's a very fitting name. Was that your idea?"

"Me? No, I'm not a fan of animated shows. It was my nephew, Demetrius. *The Simpsons* is his favorite show. You should see his impression of Ned Flanders."

"Oh, I get it now." I point at Xander's donkey.

"That's why he's called Bart and why my aunt is riding a donkey names Marge. Speaking of, where is she?"

"She's probably already at the site." He puts his hand over his eyes to shield them from the sun and looks up the path. "We're not that far. Do you want to walk the rest of the way with me?"

"Sure, anything to keep a little distance between Mr. Stinky and myself for a while." After dismounting, I hand Xander my reins, being careful to make sure Homer doesn't mistake the pants I'm wearing as a potential snack.

While we meander up the path, I ask Xander what his favorite television show is.

"Let's see if you can guess," he says.

"What's my prize if I get it right?"

He gives me a sideways glance. "It's something you'll like."

I grab his arm and yank him to a stop. "You don't know me. You have no idea what I would like." Then I pull back, surprised by my outburst. Why does this man bring out the worst in me?

Xander stares at me with an intensity that takes my breath away. I feel my palms get sweaty, and let go of his arm. He looks down at my hand, as if just now aware that I had been touching him.

Then he shrugs. But it's no ordinary shrug, the kind where you raise your shoulders to express indifference or not knowing the answer to something.

This feels different, as though he's trying to shrug away the electricity between us.

I mentally shake myself. My aunt was right. I have been hate-flirting with Xander and he's been doing the same back. This is so unlike me on so many levels.

Xander looks off into the distance for a moment. When he speaks again, it's with a matter-of-fact tone, one you would use with a stranger. "You're right. We don't know each other. That's why you'll never guess what my favorite TV show is."

"Don't be so cocky."

"I'm not being cocky," he says. "Just realistic. How many TV shows have been made over the years? Billions?"

"Billions might be a stretch," I say. "But I'll concede that there are a lot of shows."

He smirks. "You should probably give up now."

"Never." I grin when I realize we're hate-flirting again. "I'm curious to find out what this prize of yours is."

Did Xander's face just redden? I try to get a closer look, but he turns and starts walking our donkeys up the path. "Come on, let's catch up with Celeste," he says over his shoulder.

We walk the rest of the way in silence. I glance at Xander from time to time, trying to figure out what he likes to watch on TV. This mysterious prize of his has to be a kiss, right? What would those lips of his feel like . . .

Stop it! I tell myself. *Stop thinking about Xander that way. Nothing can happen with this man. Nothing.*

I straighten my shoulders, take a deep breath, and remind myself that Xander is short for Alexander. As in Alexander Papadakis, the man I have to charm into selling his property to my company. If there's one thing that Frank's drilled into my head, it's that you never mix business with pleasure.

My mood darkens as the path continues up the hill. I'm not cut out for this cloak and dagger stuff. Frank makes it look easy—he's turned backstabbing into an art form. He's so good at smooth talking that people don't even feel the knife slipping in.

"I thought I was going to have to send out a search party," Aunt Celeste says when she spots us.

"Sorry," I say. "Homer doesn't seem to be on the same schedule as the rest of us."

"Don't worry about it. I've been enjoying the view." She winks at us. "I'm glad the two of you got some alone time."

Xander smiles at her, then offers to set up the picnic lunch. "Don't worry, Olivia. I brought food that even the pickiest eater will enjoy. Cheese, bread, and fruit. Or is fruit too healthy for you?"

I roll my eyes. "I like healthy food."

"Tacos don't count," he says.

"Nine out of ten nutritionists recommend that you eat a taco a day."

He laughs. "Are those the same nutritionists who

think soft serve is the same thing as ice cream?"

"Olivia loves soft serve." My aunt looks at me. "You're always saying that's the best part of your job, all the soft serve you can eat."

"What exactly do you do?" Xander asks.

My eyes widen. I have no idea what to say. How come I don't have a cover story prepared?

I chew on my bottom lip. "I'm uh, a . . ."

My aunt shoots me a look, then says, "Olivia has a really interesting job. She—"

I quickly cut her off. "It's actually pretty boring. I train people on computer systems. Now, what about that lunch?"

Xander nods, then busies himself unpacking the saddle bags.

While he sets up our lunch, my aunt leads me over to look at one of the ruins. "What was that all about?" she asks when we're out of earshot. "Why are you hiding what you do for a living from Xander?"

"I told him the truth," I say. "I do systems training."

"Oh, please, that's a small part of your job," Celeste says. "Why didn't you tell him that you're responsible for getting operations up and running at new Humpty Dumpty resorts? I think he'd be impressed."

I shake my head. "No, he wouldn't."

"I think you're wrong. Xander has an MBA from Harvard," my aunt informs me. "Until recently, he worked for a large multinational company. I'm sure he'd be very interested in hearing about your career. The two of you probably have a lot in common."

I grab my aunt's arm—partly to keep her from calling Xander over to talk shop and partly to keep from myself collapsing on the ground. I feel faint. Why didn't Frank tell me about Xander's background? This isn't a man that can be easily fooled into making a deal with the Humpty Dumpty corporation.

"Olivia, are you okay?" Concern is etched on my aunt's brow. "You're white as a sheet."

When I see Xander walking over to us, I say, "Whatever you do, don't tell Xander what I do or who I work for. I'll explain later." Then I force a smile on my face and turn to Xander. "Is the picnic ready?"

CHAPTER 6
UNIBROWS AND EXTRA BRAIN CELLS

"Hurry up, Olivia," Aunt Celeste says as she peeks her head into my room the next night. "We're going to be late for dinner."

I'm standing in front of the mirror, holding up two tops. One of them is a silk shirt that I normally wear with my dark gray suit. The other is an embroidered peasant-style blouse that I bought at a local store yesterday, along with a few other casual clothing items. Except for a quick shopping trip, my aunt and I had spent the day relaxing by the pool. Well, Aunt Celeste relaxed, spending her time doing yoga, reading magazines, and attempting to do a watercolor painting of Midnight. Turns out cats aren't the most cooperative when it comes to sitting for a portrait. Midnight thought knocking over the jar of water Aunt

Celeste used to clean her brushes was far more fun than having his likeness captured.

When I wasn't trying to wrangle the cat, I pretended to relax. When my aunt asked me why I was spending so much time on my laptop, I told her I was playing video games. Fortunately, she bought that excuse because, in reality, I was working on a cost analysis and project plan report for Frank.

Now, after having secretly put in a full day's work, I have to go have dinner at the taverna with my aunt and Xander. I can't believe I got talked into this. I would much rather stay here at the villa and eat a grilled cheese sandwich, but my aunt has her heart set on having spanakopita tonight.

I lean forward and look at my eyes in the mirror. Ugh. These dark circles are Frank's fault. Staying up late working on stuff for him and then not being able to fall asleep because I'm so worried about Xander finding out what I do for a living is starting to take a toll.

"What's the holdup?" my aunt asks.

I turn toward her. "I can't decide what to wear."

"That one." Aunt Celeste points at the peasant blouse. "It suits your complexion."

"Don't you think it's too garish?" I examine the blouse more closely, wondering how anyone would have the patience to embroider such an intricate pattern.

"Garish? Not at all. It's fun and playful. Unlike your

boring work clothes." Celeste grabs the silk shirt from me and makes a point of placing it into my suitcase. Then she goes to my closet, pulls out the rest of my business clothes, then tosses them in as well.

Midnight must somehow sense that my suitcase is open, because he rushes into my room and promptly jumps inside. As he rolls around on my work clothes, Celeste smiles. "Good kitty. If you shed enough cat hair on them, then Olivia won't be able to wear those dreadful outfits."

I feel my face flush. Does she really think my clothes are dreadful? I go to a lot of trouble to make sure that I'm always dressed in a polished and professional manner. My suits were perfectly tailored in black, navy blue, or varying shades of gray. My clothes are meant to project a competent, business-like persona, not give off vacation vibes.

As if reading my mind, my aunt pats my arm. "Maybe dreadful was a bit harsh. You're an impeccable dresser, your hair is always styled perfectly, and I don't think I've ever seen you when your face isn't made up flawlessly, but . . ."

While Aunt Celeste pauses to consider her next words carefully, I shoo Midnight out of my suitcase. I hang my clothes back up in my closet, silently cursing the cat for getting hair over all of them. Glancing back at my aunt, I ask, "But what?"

"Honestly, dear, your look is a bit boring." She sits down on my bed and strokes the disgruntled cat. "I remember when you were little. You wore the most outrageous outfits that you'd make for yourself out of odds and ends."

Celeste chuckles. "My favorite was your alien octopus dishwasher repairer. You used a box of aluminum foil, a mop, and raided your dad's closet. At first, he was horrified when he saw what you had done with his ties, but you looked so adorable that he couldn't be mad for long."

"He wouldn't let me use scissors for a month after that," I say.

"What happened to that girl?" Celeste asks. "The one who was spontaneous and always giggling."

"Grown women don't giggle," I say.

"Speak for yourself. I giggle all the time." Celeste smiles softly. "Except maybe after your Uncle Ernie died. It was hard to find a reason to smile, let alone giggle, for a long time."

I sit on the bed next to her and squeeze her hand. "The two of you were so lucky to have each other."

"We were. He was so cute. He'd always say, 'Can I borrow a kiss? I promise I'll give it back to you.' And he always did, with interest." Aunt Celeste gets a faraway look in her eyes. After a few moments, she turns back to me and gives me a sly smile. "I'm sure you'll meet your special someone soon. In fact, you may have already met him."

"Are you talking about Xander?"

"Have you met any other men on this island I don't

know about?"

"Of course not." I walk back to the mirror and touch up my eyeliner. "And, for the record, there's nothing going on between Xander and me."

"Not yet, you mean. Admit it, dear, you're attracted to him, and it's obvious he's attracted to you."

"The man has a unibrow," I point out.

"You know that's a sign of intelligence, right? Those hairs between the eyebrows are a side effect of all the extra brain cells they have."

I burst out laughing. My aunt is so goofy sometimes. "I suppose you read about that in a scientific journal?"

"Correct. There was also an article in the same journal about how women who dressed up as alien octopus dishwasher repairers when they were little girls are seven times more likely to be attracted to men with unibrows."

"Wow, it's amazing the types of scientific studies that get funding these days."

"Unibrows are all the rage in academic circles these days." She chuckles, then her expression sobers. "I still don't understand why you want me to keep what you do for a living secret from Xander."

I sigh. "It's complicated."

"I can handle complicated."

"Maybe complicated isn't the right word. It's more that . . ." My voice trails off as I try to figure out how to explain the situation to my aunt. Why am I reluctant to tell her about what I'm working on for Frank? I've always been up front with her . . . until now.

A small voice nags at the back of my head. *Maybe it's because you're scared of how she'll react. Maybe it's because she'll tell you that what you're doing is wrong.*

I push those thoughts aside. This is how business is done. You have to keep secrets, otherwise your competitors would edge you out. Frank is constantly telling me that I need to toughen up if I want to get ahead. This is my opportunity to prove that I have what it takes to play in the big league. And that means keeping some things to myself.

I change into the peasant blouse, then tell my aunt a half-truth. "My company's HR Director was emphatic that I shouldn't think about work while I'm on vacation. She thinks it's important that I focus on relaxing so that I can recharge my batteries. I can't really unplug effectively if I talk with Xander about my job. We should stick with other topics, like why his donkey smells worse than a boys' locker room."

From the expression on my aunt's face, I don't think she believes me. I'm not sure I believe me either.

* * *

When we walk into the taverna an hour later, Athena puts her hands on her hips, narrows her eyes, and glares at Aunt Celeste. I take a few steps to the side. A person could catch on fire if they got in the way of the death rays coming out of the older Greek woman's eyes. Or worse, they could be hit with a glob of spit.

My aunt doesn't seem to notice the other woman. "I think that's our table over there," Aunt Celeste says breezily to me. The room goes silent as she marches across the tiled floor to the far end of the restaurant. Athena trails behind her, brandishing an evil eye and muttering something under her breath. The other patrons look up from their meals, clearly intrigued by the drama.

"Come on, dear," Aunt Celeste says over her shoulder to me as she sits down.

Athena spins around to see who my aunt is talking to. When she spots me, Athena points a bony finger in my direction. "You're with her?"

"I'm sorry," I say with what I hope sounds like a Canadian accent.

Athena appears momentarily mollified by my apology. She starts to say something to me, but a loud clanging noise coming from the direction of the kitchen distracts her. When she rushes off to investigate, I scurry over to join my aunt. I do my best not to make eye contact with the other patrons. Being the center of attention is so embarrassing.

"Athena really can't let go of whatever her beef is

with me," Aunt Celeste says as I sit down.

"Tell me again why you thought it was a good idea to eat here?" I ask.

"It was Xander's suggestion. He wants to be a peacemaker. Isn't that sweet?" She shakes her head. "I'm more than happy to let bygones by bygones, but it's apparent Athena can't let go."

"I wish you'd tell me what happened between you two."

"Later, I promise. Right now, I want to enjoy our dinner, not rehash unpleasant memories."

I look around the taverna. Thankfully, Athena hasn't reappeared, and with the floor show over, the other diners have stopped looking in our direction.

"How do you know this is our table?" I rub the back of my neck, wondering if we should have waited to be seated. I don't want to give Athena another reason to be upset.

"Do you remember how you admired the wildflowers when we were at the archaeological site?" My aunt points at the vase on the table. "These are the same ones."

My stomach flutters as I recall how Xander had picked a small bouquet for me that day. My old boyfriend used to send me flowers on a weekly basis. Correction, he had his secretary send them. They were always red roses. I'm not a huge fan of roses, but I could never muster up the courage to tell him. It was easier just to smile and graciously say thank you.

Although they cost nothing, Xander's bouquet of wildflowers touched me more than my ex-boyfriend's expensive roses.

"I think Xander picked these flowers just for you," my aunt says.

I shake my head. "I don't think he'd go to all that trouble for me."

Aunt Celeste arches an eyebrow. "I think that man would go to a lot of trouble for you."

"Even if he did pick them, it's not a big deal. They probably grow like weeds around here. It means nothing."

"These particular flowers are rare. They only grow in the fields near the archaeological site. Remember how we read about it in that guidebook yesterday?"

"Are you saying he went back up there today to get these?" I pull the vase toward me for a better look. "That's a pretty long walk just for flowers."

"He didn't do it for the flowers. He did it for you."

"Surely Xander has better things to do with his time."

I startle as a hand rests on my shoulder. It's Xander. It has to be. How else do you explain the goosebumps I'm feeling as fingers lightly brush the nape of my neck?

"What should I be doing with my time?" he asks. "I'm all ears."

"Be on time," I say primly. "My aunt and I have been waiting for you."

I know. It's a lame response, but I'm horrible at hate-flirting.

What? Hate-flirting? Where did that come from? I'm not hate-flirting. I'm not doing flirting of any kind.

When Xander removes his hands from my shoulders, I feel something that I don't know how to describe. It's an absence of some sort. It's like a connection was severed and my skin aches for it to be reestablished.

I watch as Xander walks around the table, then bends down to kiss my aunt on each cheek. For some reason, I'm offended that he hasn't greeted me in a similar fashion. Where's my kiss? I want to shout at him.

"You're the ones who are late, even by Greek standards," Xander says as he sits next to my aunt. "I've been here at the taverna for hours preparing your dinner."

His words remind me that I barely know anything about Greek culture. The Humpty Dumpty corporation prides itself on creating a comfortable American ambiance at its resorts. If I'm honest, our guests like saying that they've traveled to foreign countries, but they'd prefer to feel like they never left home. We do provide cultural experiences at our resorts, but they're carefully curated to provide just the right mix of "exotic" and "familiar."

"Apologies," my aunt says to Xander. "Olivia

couldn't decide what to wear."

"I'm glad you took your time," he says to me. "You look amazing."

His eyes linger on me, making me feel uncomfortable. I fuss with my napkin, not sure what to say or do. Fortunately, a teenage boy holding a copper pitcher approaches our table.

"This is my nephew, Demetrius," Xander says as he motions for the boy to fill our glasses. "Have you had retsina before? It's a traditional Greek wine."

"I love it," my aunt says. "But I'm not sure Olivia will like it. She's more of a diet soda kind of girl."

"I'll try it," I say quickly. Wine sounds like a really good idea right now. Maybe a drink will help me relax. Being around Xander is putting me on edge. I take a sip—well, more like a gulp—then instantly regret it.

"Is this some sort of joke? This tastes like turpentine," I blurt out.

Xander has a bemused expression on his face. "Maybe you should stick with soda. Retsina is for people with sophisticated palates."

"I'll have you know my palate is very sophisticated." And just like that, the hate-flirting is back. I feel more comfortable around Xander when we're sparring.

Xander jabs right back. "Says the woman who eats soft serve and tacos."

Aunt Celeste intervenes. "I think what he means to

say is that retsina is an acquired taste. It's made with pine resin. That's what you're tasting. The first time I tried it, I wasn't a fan. But now, I think it's the perfect accompaniment to Greek food, especially spanakopita."

"Speaking of, I should return to the kitchen." As Xander gets up from the table, he says to me, "I'll have Demetrius bring you something else to drink."

"No, I'm fine with the retsina." I choke down some more, then put on a brave smile. There's no way I'm going to let Xander think a stupid glass of wine can beat me. I'll show him. "Delicious."

"I'm so glad you like it. We make it here on the island," Xander says enthusiastically.

As he proceeds to tell us about the wine-making process, I mentally file away notes. Is this something we could adapt as a cultural experience for our guests? I think they might get a kick out of stomping grapes, then enjoying a bottle of wine on the veranda of their luxury bungalow.

I take another drink of my retsina. I think it's starting to grow on me. Or is that just the alcohol going to my head?

"We only make a small quantity of bottles of this particular retsina each year," Xander says. "And we don't sell it to outsiders."

"Thank you for sharing it with us," Aunt Celeste says.

"I want you to experience the real Greece," he

says. "This retsina represents what's so special about this island to me."

A loud clanging noise comes from the kitchen and Xander hastily excuses himself, muttering something about the dangers of leaving the cooking to others.

"He's gone. You don't have to pretend anymore," my aunt says to me.

"I'm not pretending," I say. "This retsina isn't so bad after all."

"It's nice to see that you're open to trying new things." She winks at me. "Including dating handsome Greek men."

I nearly choke on my retsina. "Who said anything about dating?"

Aunt Celeste gestures at the flowers. "This is a pretty romantic gesture."

"If he picked them, it was for *both* of us. This dinner is for *both* of us."

When my aunt suddenly closes her eyes and rubs her temples, I get suspicious. I've seen her pull this trick before when she wants to get out of situations.

"You know what, I think I'm getting a migraine," Aunt Celeste says to me. "I better go to the villa and lie down."

I give her a knowing look. "I better go with you to make sure you're all right."

"No, you stay here. Xander went to so much trouble arranging this dinner. It would be rude if both of us left."

I clutch her hand. "You can't leave me here alone."

"Trust me, you don't want me to stay. If I did, I might drink more of the retsina. Heavens knows what might come out of my mouth if I got a little tipsy. I might want to talk about your work, for example. Or the time you got suspended from school for—"

I hold my hand up. "You win. I'll stay here. You go back to the villa."

"Enjoy your date," she says as she blows me a kiss.

"It's not a date," I call out after her. "I would never go on a date with Xander. He has a unibrow, for goodness' sake."

Everyone in the taverna turns and stares at me. I really hope they don't understand English. But apparently they grasped what I said, because when Xander comes out of the kitchen, they all start laughing and pointing at the two of us. I put my head in my hands and groan. This is turning out to be the worst vacation ever.

CHAPTER 7
A PEACE OFFERING

The laughter in the room dies down as Xander looks around inquisitively. An older couple waves him over. I may not be in earshot, and I may not speak Greek, but it's obvious what they're telling Xander. Something along the lines of, "That crazy lady over there is yelling about the two of you and dating."

Xander has the decency to look embarrassed while he's talking to the couple. But as he walks over to my table, he flashes me a cocky grin.

"Apparently you told everyone that we're dating," he says smugly when he joins me.

"No, I clearly said that we're *not* dating."

"But you mentioned 'dating' and me in the same sentence." He leans down and whispers in my ear, "That's your subconscious' way of saying that you want to date me."

I pull away. "Why would I want to date you? You're arrogant and full of yourself."

"Arrogant and full of myself—aren't those the same thing?"

"I was making a point." I grab my purse. "And now I'm going to go back to the villa and check on my aunt."

Worry flashes across Xander's face. "Is she okay?"

"She's pretending to have a migraine." When I realize what I've said, I put a hand over my mouth.

"A *pretend* migraine," Xander says slowly. "English may not be my first language, but I do know that means she's not really sick. No reason for you to go back to the villa then and ruin our date."

I push my chair back and get up from the table, but before I can storm out of the taverna, Xander grabs me gently by the shoulders.

"I was kidding," he says. "Of course, this isn't a date. It's just two friends having dinner."

"We're not friends," I say firmly.

"I have a feeling you don't have many friends," Xander says softly. "Maybe you could use one."

I feel my eyes water as his words hit too close to home. It's true. Work keeps me so busy that most of my high school and college friendships have faded away. We exchange Christmas cards and like each other's social media posts, but that's about it. I probably only have one close friend left, but between

Jasmine's schedule and the demands of my job, we don't get to talk much.

"Stay, Olivia." Xander pulls me closer to him. "Have some more retsina, try my spanakopita, and, who knows, maybe by the end of the evening, you might bring yourself to call me a friend."

A lone tear drips down my face, and when Xander dabs it with a napkin, I lose it. "Excuse me, I need to . . ." I don't finish my sentence. I'm so choked up that I couldn't speak even if I wanted to. I rush to the bathroom, lock myself inside, then slump on the floor and start sobbing.

I don't know how much time passes, but eventually, I'm all cried out. When I get up and look at myself in the mirror, I groan. Who is the woman staring back at me? She has the same hair, eyes, and coloring as I do, but the expression on her face is unfamiliar. It's like she's given up.

"Go away," I say when I hear someone knocking on the door. I splash water on my face, then instantly regret it when my mascara and eyeliner smears. I dab at it with a paper towel while I try to figure out how I'm going to get out of this bathroom without Xander seeing me. There's a window, but it's too small for me to climb out of. Maybe I can just stay in here until the taverna closes?

The knock at the door becomes more insistent. Fine. I wipe off my smudged makeup. I might as well get this over with. Steeling myself to face Xander, I pull the door open with all the dignity I can muster. But instead of seeing the man who brought me to tears, I'm face-to-face with Athena.

"Are you okay, darlin'?" she asks with that faint Texan twang of hers.

Her tone is so gentle and kind that I'm confused. This can't be the same woman who yelled and spit at my aunt. Does she have a twin?

"I'm fine," I say. "I think I ate something that disagreed with me."

"But you haven't eaten anything," she points out. "Xander hadn't served the spanakopita yet."

"Maybe it was the retsina," I say.

She dismisses my theory. "It was Xander. You're not the first woman he's done this to."

"What do you mean?" I clench the paper towel in my hands.

Athena looks down at the floor and clears her throat. That's when I realize I've torn the towel into shreds. "Sorry about that," I say as I pick the pieces up and deposit them in the trash.

"I'm always telling Xander to be more serious, but does he listen? No." Athena jabs a finger in my direction. "He flirts with girls who are entirely inappropriate."

My jaw drops. Who is she calling inappropriate?

Athena seems to realize the effect her words have on me. She lowers her hand, then says in a less strident tone, "It's because he spent too much time in the States. There are days when I can't tell if he's American or Greek. Everyone on the island thinks the same thing."

"What's wrong with being American?"

"They're loud and pushy. You remember those frat boys who were in here the other day? They were so obnoxious."

I wring my hands together. "Do you think I'm loud and pushy?"

"Of course not. You're a sweet Canadian girl. Which is why I don't understand why you would be friends with Celeste. She's the epitome of an obnoxious American."

I take a deep breath. It's confession time. I can't continue to deceive Athena. Partly because I'm scared of her and partly because all the lying isn't sitting easily on my conscience. Looking the older woman in the eye, I say, "I'm actually American. And Celeste is my aunt."

A mix of anger and confusion flashes across the older woman's face. "I don't believe that."

"It's true. I'm staying with my aunt at her villa."

She shakes her head. "You were born in Canada. Somehow you got switched with an American baby at birth. That's the only logical explanation."

"I'm sorry I lied to you, really I am. But I'm one-hundred percent American."

"But how do you explain the Canadian money in your purse and your accent?"

"I worked in Canada," I explain. "I spent a lot of time there, which probably explains why I sound a bit Canadian. I tend to pick up accents when I'm in a place for a while."

Athena purses her lips. "I hope you and your aunt aren't a bad omen that our island is going to be overrun with American tourists. We like things the way they are. A few polite and quiet visitors each year who respect our culture and traditions."

"But more tourists would be good for the island's economy," I say.

"It would change our way of life. I've seen it happen in other parts of Greece." She sniffs. "That's a price we're not willing to pay."

It's not worth arguing with her. "Is Xander still here?" I ask. "I should probably go back to the villa, but I don't want to run into him."

"When I saw you rush in here, I told him to leave." She pats my arm. "You seem like a nice girl despite your country of birth. Let me pack up the spanakopita for you to take back."

As I walk out of the taverna with my takeout container, I do my best to ignore the hushed conversations and sideways looks from the other patrons. I vow never to come back to this taverna again. Or to this island, for that matter. Thankfully, my fake vacation will be over soon.

Once outside, I pause for a moment to take in my surroundings. I breathe in the night air and then try to breathe out the tension in my body. It's not easy. Usually, when I feel knots in my shoulders, it's because Frank is pressuring me to meet a deadline. That's still a contributing factor—there are a dozen texts on my phone from Frank—but there's more to it this time. Athena has made it clear what she thinks about mass tourism. I'm so glad she doesn't know about the work I'm doing for the Humpty Dumpty corporation. She certainly wouldn't think I was such a nice girl then, would she?

And then there's Xander. If I'm honest with myself, I was starting to fall for him. But apparently he flirts with all sorts of inappropriate girls. He's definitely not the kind of guy I need in my life.

I don't want to go back to the villa just yet. Aunt Celeste will badger me with a million questions about my "date" with Xander. The last thing I want is to tell her how I made a fool of myself by rushing into the bathroom in tears.

Something tugs at my skirt. I look down and grin when I see a familiar goat. "Houdini, you have no idea how glad I am to see you."

He bleats in response, then sets off across the plaza, pausing momentarily to make sure I'm following him. When we reach the harbor, I say, "Good idea. Let's sit here by the water for a while."

"I didn't think you wanted to see me, but okay."

I startle when I realize that Houdini hasn't suddenly learned how to speak English. No, that's a human male's voice I hear behind me. I straighten my shoulders, take a deep breath, then turn around to face the man I wish I had never met.

"No, I didn't want to see you, Xander," I say. "But since you're here, maybe we should clear the air."

* * *

As Xander and I sit on a bench, I notice he's holding a paper bag.

"It's a peace offering," he says. "Or at least it was supposed to be. I was going to wait outside the taverna and give it to you, but I chickened out."

"What is it?"

"I don't think you would have liked the spanakopita I made. All that mushy green stuff inside."

I point at the takeout container Athena gave me. "It's in here if you want it."

"Take that back to Celeste." He hands me the paper bag. "I think you'll like this better. It's a plain hamburger."

"Thank you." As I pull the burger out, my stomach grumbles in anticipation.

"It's cold," Xander warns me.

"That's okay. I'm starving." I start to eat it, then hesitate. "What's this made out of?"

Xander chuckles. "Beef."

"I think this is the most delicious hamburger I've

ever had," I say in between bites. "Where did you get it?"

"It's a secret," he says. "Wouldn't want word to get out and have millions of tourists flocking to our island."

As he says that, I feel sick to my stomach. Little does he know that if the Humpty Dumpty corporation gets its way, people will be flocking to this island. I crumple up the wrapper and place it in the bag.

He takes it from me and throws it in a nearby trashcan. When he sits back down, he grins at me. "If only I had known it would be so easy to win your heart."

I try to match his light-hearted tone. "It's my taste buds you've won over, not my heart."

"I'll take it. Small wins add up over time."

"There's not much time left. My vacation is over at the end of next week." I chew on my bottom lip and stare out at the harbor. What a stupid thing to say. As if I want him to win over my heart before I leave. Especially since I'm such an inappropriate woman.

When Xander takes my hand, I flinch. "What's wrong?" he asks.

"Just something Athena said."

Xander releases my hand and says something sharply in his native tongue. Then he turns back to me. "Sorry, I don't normally swear in front of ladies."

"Don't worry, it was all Greek to me."

That gets a smile out of Xander. Then he turns

serious. "What did she say to you?"

"It doesn't matter."

"It matters to me." Houdini looks up from where he's resting and bleats loudly. Xander laughs. "Apparently, it matters to him as well."

"She said that you have a history of flirting with inappropriate women." Xander starts to speak, but I cut him off. "While I don't like what she said, Athena did make me realize that whatever this is between us is foolish. You live on Gáidaros and I live in the States. Nothing can come out of this."

Xander arches an eyebrow. "First of all, this 'history' of mine is a bunch of nonsense. I haven't been interested in a woman for a long, long time. Second, I'll be the judge of who's appropriate for me." He takes my hand in his again. "Despite the fact that you have the taste buds of a five-year-old, I still think you're the epitome of appropriate for me."

"Even though I'm American?"

"What does that have to do with anything?"

"Athena isn't too fond of Americans. I'm guessing other folks on Gáidaros probably share her opinion."

Xander sighs. "She's good at putting people into boxes. It makes it easier for her, you know."

"What do you mean?"

"Oh, it's a long story," he says. "And it's not really mine to tell. Suffice it to say that you should take what she says with a grain of salt. Anyway, I try to look for what people have in common, not focus on their differences." He leans against the back of the bench and points upwards. "I like to think about the fact that we're all under the same sky, looking up at the same moon."

"It's a nice sentiment," I say. "But—"

Xander puts his finger on my lips and shushes me. "Enough of this serious talk. You know what we need? Ice cream. Real ice cream." As he pulls me to my feet, he says, "Let me guess. Vanilla is your favorite flavor."

"Yep. It's simple and straightforward." I grin. "I bet yours is rocky road. Dark and complicated."

"Not even close. I like strawberry."

"You don't strike me as the kind of guy who likes pink food."

"I had a sister who loved the color pink. I guess it rubbed off on me." He grabs my hand. "Come on, let's get going before they close."

It isn't until we near the ice cream shop when two important things hit me. First, we're holding hands while we walk, and it feels like the most natural thing in the world. Second, and more importantly, Xander referred to his sister in the past tense. I want to ask him about it, but something holds me back. It's something he'll need to share with me in his own time.

"Give me a sec," Xander says as he holds the door open. "I need to call my mom."

"You don't look happy about it."

"She wants me to do something I really don't want to do. When she gets fixated on an idea, there's no stopping her." He sighs. "I know she has my best interests at heart, but honestly, sometimes she's too much. Know what I mean?"

"Not really. My mom is pretty laid back." I smile as I think about my parents. "She's always quick to laugh and enjoys nothing more than playing practical jokes. Dad, on the other hand, is the serious, responsible one. Guess which one I take after?"

"Well, you're on vacation now. That means more laughing is in order." He gently pushes me inside. "Go get your vanilla ice cream. I'll join you in a minute."

While he talks with his mom on the phone, I contemplate the ice cream choices. Maybe I'll surprise Xander and myself and get something completely out of character. Rocky road it is.

CHAPTER 8
ANOTHER DONKEY RIDE

How the heck did I end up riding a donkey again? Oh, yeah, I remember. Last night, over ice cream, Xander conned me into this. He convinced me that unless I visited an olive grove, my trip to Greece would be incomplete. I tried to tell him that I hate olives. They have a disturbing texture, kind of like how I imagine slugs would taste. He laughed, telling me that he would bring peanut butter and jelly sandwiches for me to eat.

Predictably, Aunt Celeste had another one of her fake migraines this morning. So it's just me and Xander today. Thankfully, when Xander showed up this morning, he brought a new donkey for me to ride. I laughed when he told me his name—Mr. Ed. The poor fellow probably has a complex being named after a horse, and a celebrity television-star horse at that.

"It won't be long now," Xander says over his shoulder.

Like last time, he's walking alongside his donkey while I'm riding mine. Mr. Ed and I trail behind on the narrow path. I have to give props to Mr. Ed. Unlike Homer, he doesn't stop every five minutes to nibble on grass and rocks, and, more importantly, I haven't smelled one single donkey fart since we set out.

There's been an easy kind of silence between Xander and me today, which I appreciate. My last boyfriend never stopped talking. It would have been one thing if he discussed interesting things with me, but it was always a one-sided conversation and it always revolved around him. How much his last bonus was, how great he was at tennis, the time he was an extra in a Star Wars movie, that sort of thing.

After a while, I figured out that it didn't matter if I actually paid attention to what he said. All I had to do was nod and occasionally say, "That's great, babe." In exchange, he took me out to fancy dinners and had his secretary send me roses. I'd say he got the better end of the bargain.

I broke up with him via email. Know what his response was? "Thanks for the update. All the best in your future endeavors." Ever since then, I've *endeavored* to stay single. It hasn't been hard. Guys don't generally ask me out.

As if reading my mind, Xander turns around again. "Do you want to go hear traditional Greek music with me tomorrow night?"

While I consider how to reply, it hits me. We've stopped hate-flirting. Ever since our heart-to-heart last night, we've stopped slinging sarcastic zingers at each other. I think back to my conversation with Aunt Celeste this morning over breakfast.

"Ordinary flirting is a form of conversation," she said. "It makes people feel good about themselves. It doesn't always mean that you're attracted to the other person. It can just be a bit of harmless fun."

She looked at me thoughtfully while she sipped on her coffee. "But this hate-flirting that you and Xander engage in, well, that's a different beast. In my experience, that means you're really drawn to someone, but you're scared of what will happen if you get together. So you pull them toward you a little, then you push them away. Pull, push, over and over, until you finally give in to what you're feeling or you decide to walk away. My advice—be clear about what it is you're pushing away because you may regret it for the rest of your life."

"So, do you want to go hear music or not?" Xander's question jolts me back to the present.

Taking my aunt's advice to heart, I smile and say, "Sure, why not?"

After a few minutes, the olive grove comes into view. After I dismount, Xander leads the donkeys over to a small clearing and ties them up. Then he stretches his arms out. "Well, what do you think?"

My eye is drawn to the graceful rows of trees with their twisty gray bark. The tops of the trees are silhouetted by white fluffy clouds, and wildflowers add a pop of color around their roots. "It's breathtaking," I say.

Xander seems pleased with my response. "This is where I feel most myself. For too long, I chased money and promotions. I lost sight of what's really important —feeling connected to a place and its people." He looks at me and laughs. "Sorry, that sounds so cheesy."

"Not at all. It sounds genuine."

He gives me a bashful smile, then grabs my hand. "Come on, there's something I want to show you."

We stroll through the grove, stopping occasionally to look at the wildflowers more closely. He picks a few for me, and I tuck them behind my ear.

"Wow, what's that?" I ask when we come face-to-face with a large, almost magical-looking tree with twisty, gnarled bark and roots. I'm not sure if Greece has wood fairies, but if it does, I'd expect them to live here.

"This is the oldest olive tree in all of Greece," Xander says.

I furrow my brow as I remember something I read in a guidebook at the villa. "I thought that was on the island of Crete. It's something like three thousand years old."

"Never trust what you read in a guidebook. The tree you see in front of you is much older."

I snort in disbelief. "I find that hard to believe. Those are olives growing on it, right? How could anything that old still be producing fruit?"

"Fruit, huh? I thought you were convinced olives were the plant equivalent of slugs."

"Don't get technical with me."

"I don't think you can handle technical."

Listening to us, you might think we're back to hate-flirting, but there's a tangible difference in our dialog. Not the least of which is the fact that Xander is stroking my cheek. He lightly traces his fingers down my face, then presses his fingertips ever so slightly on my neck. If he can feel my pulse, he'll know that it's racing.

"Yoo-hoo!" a voice calls out.

I reluctantly step back from Xander and look at the familiar-looking couple walking toward us. They're both wearing sturdy hiking boots and waving walking sticks in the air.

"I told you that's the girl we met on the ferry," the woman says to her husband.

"When you're right, you're right," he says cheerfully.

"Where's your manners, luv," she says. "Introduce us."

The man holds out his hand to Xander. "G'day. Noah and Amelia Hornsby from Down Under at your service."

After we finish introductions, the Hornsbys tell us about how many kilometers they've walked since they arrived on the island.

"You won't catch us riding a donkey," Noah says. "There's a reason why God gave us these two feet."

Amelia nods. "That's right, luv. Feet are for walking, not for lazing about in stirrups."

Xander clears his throat. "Actually—"

I interrupt before he can tell the Hornsbys about my donkey ride. "Did you know this is the oldest olive tree in Greece?"

"We sure do," Amelia says. "That's why we came up here to get a look at it before it gets chopped down."

Xander's jaw drops. "Chopped down? What are you talking about?"

"Maybe they won't use an ax," Amelia says. "They might just bulldoze it down."

"This is private property," Xander says. "*My* private property. No one is going to come up here with an ax or bulldozer without my permission."

Noah lets out a long whistle. "Sonny, they'll do what they always do. Throw a ton of money at you, and you'll sign over your land without a peep."

Xander throws his hands in the air. "Will one of you please tell me what's going on?"

"Not everyone reads the financial news every morning like you do, luv," Amelia says to Noah. Then she turns to Xander. "There was a story today about how the Humpty Dumpty corporation is planning on opening a resort on a Greek island near Rhodes. Humpty Dumpty's CEO declined to comment on the story. However, there's widespread speculation that they want to build here, on Gáidaros."

Xander narrows his eyes and mutters something under his breath. I'm pretty sure it's the same Greek swear word he uttered while we were at the harbor last night. Maybe I'm learning how to speak Greek after all.

When Xander regains his composure, Noah shows him the story on his phone, which, of course, causes him to lose his composure again. While the three of them have an animated discussion about the ramifications of building a resort on Gáidaros, I send Frank a text asking him what's going on.

He replies within seconds:

I could ask you the same thing. Are you the leak?

I'm too stunned to text back right away. How could he think I would share confidential information with the press?

Frank sends another text. This one's short and sweet:

Well?

I try to type a response, but my cell phone screen doesn't respond to my touch. Probably because it's covered with a thick layer of sweat from my hands. I wipe the screen off with the bottom of my shirt, then try again:

Absolutely not. I'm a loyal egg.

Yes, Humpty Dumpty employees are referred to as "eggs." If you're promoted to the management team, people congratulate you on your "hatching."

Even though we're on two different continents, I can sense Frank's panic. Our Chief Rooster—that's CEO in Humpty Dumpty speak—has probably called Frank into his office. "For cluck's sake," the Chief Rooster would have said to my boss. "Salvage the situation immediately or you'll be a rotten egg."

Frank would have been quaking in his boots. The last person deemed to be a "rotten egg" was fired on the spot. From his next text, I can tell that he's looking for someone to blame:

Your shell is going to crack if we don't close this deal.

My hands shake as I send Frank a text assuring him I have everything under control.

"Olivia, are you okay?" Xander asks. "You're white as a sheet."

I shove my phone in my pocket. "Just thinking about the Humpty Dumpty story."

"I really hope they don't get a foothold on this island," Amelia says. "Funny how their press releases never mention the environmental destruction their construction projects cause."

"That can't be right," I say. "They have

environmental mitigation plans in place."

"Don't believe everything you read on their website." Noah points at the old olive tree. "That will be in their way, so they'll chop it down."

Amelia looks at Xander. "They'll leave your local economy in tatters."

I furrow my brow. "But Humpty Dumpty resorts create jobs. That has to be good for the economy."

"Low-paying jobs," Amelia says. "And don't think that the local stores, bars, or restaurants will benefit. Humpty Dumpty's guests spend all of their time and money on site at the resort. Any souvenirs they buy are from Humpty Dumpty gift shops. Their drinks and food come from Humpty Dumpty bars and restaurants. All the money earned on this island goes straight back into Humpty Dumpty's pockets."

"I don't know why anyone bothers going to their resorts," Noah says. "They might as well stay back in America. While they're at the resort, they eat the same type of food they get back home."

Amelia shakes her head. "Can you believe they serve tacos and hamburgers in those places? Seriously, who would go to a foreign country just to eat the same food they can have back home?"

Xander chuckles. "Olivia likes tacos and hamburgers."

"Sure, who doesn't?" Amelia says. "But when you're traveling, you eat the local cuisine, right?"

I'm feeling a weird mixture of embarrassment and

irritation. What's wrong with wanting to eat familiar food? Why are they hating on Americans who like to go to Humpty Dumpty resorts? It's a stress-free way to enjoy your vacation. You don't have to plan anything and there aren't any surprises.

Perhaps Noah senses my discomfort because he nudges his wife, then says, "Maybe we're being too hard on those types of folks. Just because we don't like that type of vacation doesn't mean it's not right for others."

"I suppose." Amelia holds up her hands. "But Humpty Dumpty is different from other resort chains. The only thing that's important to them is the bottom line."

Noah grins. "Which is why we're going to keep them off this island."

Xander stares at the other man. "We?"

"Amelia and I love a good protest," Noah says. "I'm sure Olivia will pitch in."

"Why don't we all meet at the taverna tomorrow?" Amelia suggests. "We can put our heads together and come up with a plan."

"Perfect," Xander says. "That will give me time to enlist support from others on the island."

"But what about going to hear music?" I ask.

Xander shakes his head. "This is way more important."

After discussing logistics, Noah and Amelia head off, and it's just Xander and me. When he puts his arm around my shoulders and thanks me for helping save his island, my eyes water. This isn't going to end well. Either I betray Xander by helping my boss build a Humpty Dumpty resort on his beloved island, or I stand by Xander and lose my job in the process.

Then, when I think things couldn't get any worse, Xander kisses me.

CHAPTER 9
LIFE LESSONS FROM A CAT

As soon as Xander's lips touch mine, I panic.

No, this can't be happening. I'm an egg. A good egg. A loyal egg. Only rotten eggs mix business with pleasure.

Focus on work, I tell myself. Think about project plans and spreadsheets. Anything to take your mind off Xander's lips.

I try to picture the latest customer satisfaction survey results in my head. Seventy-eight percent of our guests said that they prefer mild taco sauce, fourteen percent like hot sauce, and only eight percent think tacos should be sauce-free. I wonder if any of them would think a gyros was an acceptable substitute for a taco.

Okay, that didn't help. Thinking about Greek food

reminds me that there's a Greek guy kissing me. Xander is utterly distracting. Would it really be that bad if I mixed business with pleasure?

And believe me, there's a lot of pleasure going on here. Xander's lips are soft and rough at the same time. How can something be both soft and rough? No idea, but the sensation is amazing. He trails kisses down my neck while twining his fingers in my hair. Then his hands run down my back. He draws me closer to him and murmurs something in Greek.

My heart races. I can't understand what he's saying, but that doesn't matter. The meaning is clear —he wants me. From the way my body reacts to his, he knows that I want him too.

Xander suddenly pulls back and looks at me intently. He starts to say something, but I silence him with my lips. I start off with light, teasing kisses, then ratchet up the intensity until he moans softly.

He takes charge again, pressing me against a tree. When he nips my earlobe, it sends me over the edge. Then the panic bubbles up again and I push him away.

"We can't do this, Xander." I pace back and forth, quietly muttering the lyrics to the Humpty Dumpty company song over and over like a mantra. *Scrambled eggs, fried eggs, eggs any way you please. Poached eggs, hard boiled eggs, eggs any way you like them. We're eggtastic, you're eggtastic, let's have a yolk good time.*

It doesn't have the calming influence I hoped for. Instead, it reminds me of my quandary—torn between my desire for Xander and wanting to keep my job.

The song keeps playing through my head. I press my fingers to my temples, trying to get it to stop. I slump on the ground and hug my knees to my chest. Xander sits next to me. Even though he's careful not to touch me, the heat emanating from his body makes me react physically.

"I'm sorry," he says. "I shouldn't have kissed you."

"Guess you didn't notice that I kissed you back," I say dryly.

"But I started it."

"It was going to happen regardless of who initiated it," I say. "It could have easily been me who started it."

"You can make the first move this time," he suggests playfully.

I twist my body so that I can look him in the eye. I think he assumes I'm going to kiss him because he lowers his head so that his lips are a fraction of an inch from mine.

Oh, what the heck. One more kiss can't make things any worse than they are. I close the gap between us, let go, and lose myself in the sensation.

When the intensity threatens to overwhelm us, we pull back. But that doesn't last long. The connection between us is too strong. We seek each other out over and over.

After what feels like our millionth kiss, I'm suddenly aware that something is wrong. The hair on the back of my neck is standing up, and a chill runs through me. Although Xander is currently kissing a very tantalizing spot where my left shoulder meets my neck, this isn't a reaction to him. I jump up, adopt a defensive posture, and scan my surroundings.

"Did you hear that?" My voice has a frantic edge to it. "We're not alone."

Xander slowly gets to his feet. "It was just a rooster crowing."

"What kind of rooster?" My eyes dart back and forth, trying to spot the intruder.

"I'm not sure." When the bird crows again, Xander puts his arms around me. "Are you okay, Olivia? You're shaking."

Xander's embrace has a calming influence. I feel my heart rate slow and my breathing becomes more even. I raise my head and ask, "Did you ever feel like the universe is trying to tell you something?"

When he furrows his brow, I melt. Everything about this man is sexy, even the way his dark unibrow bunches up together when he's perplexed by something.

"What do you mean?" he asks me.

"I think the rooster is a sign."

He smiles. "You're right. A rooster crowing in an olive grove—definitely a sign that we should have some kayianas."

"What's that?"

"Scrambled eggs with tomatoes and olives." When

I grimace, he laughs. "Don't worry, I'll make it without the olives just for you, my little fussy eater."

Now it's my turn to furrow my brow. How do I explain to Xander that we can't be together? The rooster wasn't a sign that we should eat eggs, but rather a reminder of my job at the Humpty Dumpty corporation.

"You're sweet. But this isn't about food." I take a deep breath, let it out slowly, then say, "This is about us."

His jaw tightens. "What about us?"

"I like you a lot, but . . ." My voice trails off as I struggle to figure out what to say. I can't tell him the truth, that's for sure.

"I know what this is about," Xander says.

"You do?"

He nods. "You're here on vacation. You view this as something temporary."

I seize on what he's said. "That's right. It won't be long before I go back to my world and you stay here on your island."

"It doesn't have to be like that," Xander says softly. "This doesn't have to end."

I take a few steps back, putting some much needed distance between us. "We have to be realistic. Long-distance relationships don't work."

"Who says it has to be long distance?"

Xander looks at me earnestly for a beat, then bends down and picks some wildflowers. When he hands the small bouquet to me, I just about die. How can I say no to this man? I've never felt this way about anyone before, and it shakes me to my core. All my life, I've always been so sure about my next steps—go to college, study hard, get a job, work hard, get promoted, work harder, and so on and so on. I've always done what was expected of me. But now, I'm wondering if that came at a cost.

The rooster crows again. I look at the flowers in my hand. Which of these is the real sign from the universe? How do I know what the right path is for me—stick with my career or throw caution to the wind for a man I just met a few days ago?

While I'm mulling this over, Xander gets a text. After he reads it, he turns to me. "That was a friend of mine in Athens. She's a management consultant and has a lot of connections in the hospitality sector. Long story short, she knows for a fact that the Humpty Dumpty corporation sent one of their top people to Gáidaros to do a feasibility study."

"I'm sure it's just a rumor," I say in a squeaky voice.

"Nope, it's true." Xander clenches his fists. "When I find out who this person is, they're going to be sorry."

* * *

"You have to tell Xander that you work for the

Humpty Dumpty corporation," Aunt Celeste says as she hands me a cup of tea the next afternoon. "If he finds out from someone else, it will be worse. And he's bound to find out. Secrets like that don't stay hidden for very long."

We're sitting at the kitchen table. I run my hands along its smooth wooden surface, admiring the warm patina. This table has been loved and cared for over the years. Like so much of what I've seen during my short time in Greece, it reflects generations of history.

The late afternoon sun is filtered through the white linen window curtains, creating a soft glow in the room. Midnight is napping on the windowsill, soaking up the heat while he dreams about whatever it is cats dream about. Shedding fur on human clothes, probably.

I envy Midnight's relaxed approach to life. Right now, I feel so tense and anxious. I'm supposed to go to the taverna tonight to meet Xander and the others for the protest meeting. Xander was silent on our trip back from the olive grove yesterday, distracted by the text his friend sent him about the Humpty Dumpty spy on the island. Even the donkeys could sense his mood, moving at a much quicker pace than normal and keeping their braying to a minimum.

When we reached the villa, Xander gave me a perfunctory peck on the cheek before saying goodbye. In a way, I was glad we hadn't discussed our relationship on the way back. But that also meant that

I wasn't sure if he had gotten the message—all that kissing had been a mistake. By now, I knew without a doubt what the universe had been trying to tell me with the rooster crowing—Xander and I do not have a future together. End of story.

"Olivia, are you listening to me?" my aunt asks, interrupting my train of thought. "You can't keep lying to Xander."

"Technically, I'm not lying," I say. "He's never asked if I work for the Humpty Dumpty corporation."

My aunt purses her lips. "You sound like a corrupt politician. It's a lie of omission and you know it."

I sip my tea, then pull a face. "What is this?"

"Greek mountain tea. It's brewed from the dried flowers and leaves of the sideritis plant. You might know it better as ironwort. During ancient times, it was used to heal wounds caused by iron weapons during battle." She sets a plate of cookies on the table, then gives me a meaningful look. "It's also good for mild anxiety."

"I don't think tea is going to help. My anxiety is off the charts." I nibble on one of the cookies. I think there's honey in it, but I'm beyond caring.

"You'll feel better once you tell Xander the truth." Aunt Celeste leans forward. "And not just the fact that you work for Humpty Dumpty, but the whole truth."

"What do you mean?" I furrow my brow, which, of course, makes me think about Xander's unibrow and how it perfectly frames his dark eyes. Then there are those dark eyelashes of his, the dark stubble on his chin, the small dark freckle right above his upper lip . . . and now we're getting sucked down a rabbit hole. I could get lost down here.

My aunt wags a finger at me. "You're going to tell him who you work for and how you feel about him."

"Once I tell him who I work for, he's not going to care how I feel about him," I say.

My aunt considers this for a moment. "Good point. You should lead with your feelings. Soften him up first before you do the big reveal."

"Uh-huh. Cause that wouldn't be manipulative at all." I get up and pour myself some water. I need to get the taste of ironwort out of my mouth. After I drain the glass, I turn back to my aunt. "Here's what I think I should do. End my vacation early and fly back home."

"Oh, please, you're not on vacation. You think I don't know that you've been working this entire time?"

I sink back onto my chair and absentmindedly eat another cookie. Actually, it's not bad. I think the honey is starting to grow on me. "I started out on vacation, but then my boss found out where I was staying and asked me to work on the Gáidaros project." I cock my head to one side. "Well, 'asked' isn't exactly the right word. It's more like he told me to work on it."

My aunt puts her hand over her mouth. "Oh, my

gosh. You're the spy. I knew you were working on something, but I didn't realize you were here to build a resort on this island."

"I'm not building anything," I say. "I'm working on a feasibility study, that's all."

"You'll have to explain." Aunt Celeste frowns. "I don't understand corporate-speak."

"A feasibility study is a preliminary exploration of the various factors that could affect the development of a resort. It helps management decide if they should go ahead with a project."

My aunt gives me a triumphant smile. "That's perfect."

"Huh?"

"You write a report that makes it seem like it's a bad idea to build here—which it is—and then they won't do it."

I smile at her enthusiasm. "It's not quite as simple as that. I can't just make up things."

"Why not?"

"Because they'll know if I'm lying."

"How? Are they going to send someone here to check your report?"

"That's a good question." I reach for another cookie and ponder this. Frank made it sound like I was the only one working on this report, but would he really leave something so important up to a junior employee like me? Maybe someone more senior is going to turn up any day now to check up on me.

As I wipe crumbs off my top, I shake my head. How did I get myself into this mess? I need advice about what to do next, but not from my aunt. She thinks I can fake a report and the whole problem will go away. But it's not that simple.

"Well?" My aunt taps the table. "The protest meeting starts in a couple of hours. You need to speak with Xander before then."

"You're right." I slap the table with my hand. "But first, I need to call someone."

My aunt looks amused at my outburst. "Who's that, dear?"

"My boss. For once in my life, I'm going to stand up to him."

"Fantastic!" She squeezes my hand. "It's about time you quit that job."

"Who said anything about quitting?" I chew on my bottom lip. "Actually, quitting would be easier than what I am going to say to him."

"So quit. Take the easy option."

"No way." I pinch my thumb and index finger together. "I'm this close to getting a promotion. Do you know how good it would feel to be an organic, free range Grade A egg?"

Aunt Celeste cocks her head to one side. "You've lost me."

Midnight interrupts us by jumping on the table and swishing his tail back and forth. Fur gets into my tea, but that's no great loss. When he tries to eat one of the cookies, I pull him into my lap.

"I'm taking a life lesson from the cat," I explain. "You know how dogs always bend over backwards to please people? Well, that's what I've always done with Frank. But not this time. This time, I'm going to be like a cat—direct and demanding. I'm going to tell Frank that he'll have to assign someone else to the Gáidaros project because I'm on vacation."

"From what you've told me about your boss, aren't you worried he'll go ballistic?"

"It's a risk," I say. "But I've seen my male colleagues stand up to Frank before and hold their ground. I think Frank respects them because of it."

Aunt Celeste shakes her head as she gets up to make more tea. "I hope you're right, dear."

I hope I'm right, too. I grab another cookie, wipe the fur off it, and take a bite. Usually, stress-eating helps calm my nerves, but not this time. Can I really pull off feline behavior? Or should I stick with my tried-and-true people pleasing?

CHAPTER 10
HUMAN HAIRBALLS

I have a stomachache from all the cookies I ate. Or maybe this pain in my gut is because of stress. I look at Midnight. He did shed a lot of fur when he jumped on the kitchen table. Maybe I didn't brush it all off before consuming the cookies. The knot I feel in my tummy could be a hairball. I grin. Yep, that's it. This is a sign from the universe that I'm ready to embrace my feline power and confront Frank.

While she washes the dishes, Aunt Celeste continues to pester me about Xander. "I think it's wonderful that you're going to tell your boss to take his project and shove it."

"That's not exactly how I'm going to phrase it," I say.

My aunt hands me a towel. "Do you want me to speak to him?"

I almost drop the plate I'm drying. "No. Definitely not."

She shrugs. "Okay, but if you change your mind, let me know."

"Nope, not gonna happen."

As Aunt Celeste puts the clean dishes in the cupboard, she says, "You'll feel so much better after you make that call. You'll be able to relax and enjoy the rest of your vacation with Xander."

"Once I get Frank to take me off the project, what would be the point in telling Xander about the feasibility study? It would be moot. Surely you can see the logic in that, right?"

My aunt presses her lips together. "No, I can't."

"But if I'm not involved in the resort development going forward, then it won't matter if he doesn't know," I point out.

"Of course it matters," she says. "Like I said earlier, it would be a lie of omission. And you can't build a relationship on lies."

I shake my head. "What relationship? My vacation will be over soon, and I won't ever see Xander again."

Aunt Celeste studies me for a moment. "Do you really believe that?"

"Yes," I say with more confidence than I feel. "Xander and I don't have a future together."

"If you say so. But you might find that you feel differently when it's time to leave." She dries her hands, then says, "I'll give you some privacy to call your boss."

After she leaves to go work on her watercolor painting of Midnight, I mentally prepare myself for my phone call with Frank. I run through various approaches to the conversation. Let's see, I could go with the good news / bad news scenario:

"Hey, Frank. Remember how, in my last performance review, you said that I need to be more decisive? Well, the good news is that I've made a decision. The bad news is that you're not going to like that decision."

Or I could try to lighten the mood with humor:

"Want to hear a joke, Frank? What did the doctor tell the chicken with high cholesterol? 'Lay off the eggs.' Get it? Speaking of eggs . . ."

I don't get a chance to figure out my segue from an egg joke to informing Frank I want off the project because my phone rings. My eyes widen when I see that it's the company's HR Director calling. In my experience, the HR department doesn't generally call you with good news.

"Hi, Maria," I say with forced cheerfulness. "This is a surprise."

"I'm sorry to bother you on vacation," she says to me. "But it's urgent."

I breathe a sigh of relief. If Maria is mentioning my vacation, then she doesn't know that I've been secretly working for Frank instead of relaxing.

"What's wrong?" I ask.

"This is a delicate matter," she says. "It would be

better if we could do this face-to-face. Do you mind if we do a video chat?"

"Uh, sure." I quickly look around the kitchen to see if there's anything that can incriminate me. Which is ridiculous. What do I have to hide? Okay, there's the little matter that I've been pretending to be on vacation, but, other than that, I haven't done anything wrong. Oh, my gosh, did I forget to file my monthly expense report? Is that why she's calling me?

Get a grip, I tell myself as I smooth down my hair. *Maybe some of that ironwort tea would help, after all.*

"You look great," Maria says to me once we're connected. "You've got a bit of a tan, don't you? You were looking really pale before. I'm glad you're finally getting a chance to spend some time outside getting some vitamin D instead of sitting behind a desk. Where'd you end up going for your vacation?"

I do not want to answer this question. It's already bad enough that she thinks I'm actually on vacation. I'm sure my aunt would call that another lie of omission. But there's no way I can come out and say that I'm on a Greek island. Maria is part of the senior management team. She's sure to know that Frank is working on a potential project in Greece and is bound to put two and two together.

"Someplace warm," I finally say. Then I quickly add, "You have me worried. What's going on?"

Maria takes a deep breath. "I'm just going to come

right out and say it. We've had a formal complaint filed against Frank by an employee."

"What kind of complaint?"

"It's confidential, so I can't go into the details," Maria says. "But, as you know, we take these things seriously and we've started an internal investigation."

"I'm not sure what this has to do with me."

"According to the complaint, you were a witness to the behavior in question." Maria pauses to rifle through some papers on her desk. "Do you remember the project in Australia last year and the incident with the boomerang?"

"Frank was pretty mad when that happened."

Maria looks at me sharply. "He was?"

Feeling like I've said something I shouldn't have, I splutter, "Um, maybe. I guess. I don't know."

"I need you to write a detailed report about everything that happened the day of the boomerang incident. Everything. Don't leave anything out."

I'm silent for a moment while I recall the events that transpired that day. Frank had instructed me to forget what had happened. I had managed to bury that memory until now.

"When do you need the report by?" I ask.

"Unfortunately, I need it this week," she says. "I hate to interrupt your hard-earned vacation, but your account of the events is critical for the investigation. Do you think you can do that?"

Of course, I agree to her request. How could I say

no? She doesn't know that I haven't actually had a vacation. I've spent my entire time on Gáidaros writing reports for Frank. Now I'll be writing a report about Frank. Really, in the scheme of things, what's one more report on my non-vacation?

"Thanks, Olivia. I knew I could count on you," she says. "I'll let you go so you can get started. Don't hesitate to call if you have any questions."

I start to say goodbye, but she interrupts. "Oh, and one other thing. Whatever you do, don't tell Frank about the investigation. Of course, you're on vacation, so it's not like you'll be talking to him, but just in case. Mum's the word. Okay?"

I nod in agreement and mentally add yet another lie of omission to the list.

* * *

I walk into Athena's taverna later that day with no clear plan in mind. Before my phone call with Maria, I was all set to tell Frank that I couldn't work on the feasibility study anymore. But after speaking with Maria and agreeing to write a report on the Australian boomerang incident, I'm not sure that's a good idea. I probably shouldn't take the chance. I don't want to antagonize Frank while the investigation is underway.

Maybe I should have confronted Frank after what happened with the boomerang, but I couldn't bring myself to stand up to him at the time. So I did what I always do—nothing. Thinking about my inaction makes me sick.

Looking around the taverna, I see people clamoring to stand up to a big, bad corporation and tell them to take their resort and shove it. I wish I had just a fraction of their bravery.

Xander is at the front of the restaurant, deep in conversation with a woman who appears to be in her mid-thirties. She has long dark hair which cascades down her back, sharp features, and large expressive eyes. When she hands Xander a stack of papers, she smiles at him in a way that makes me think that they're more than acquaintances. And that bothers me, big time.

Yes, I know. I told Xander that we didn't have a future together. But that doesn't mean I want him to be with anyone else. Totally selfish, I know. My mom once told me that I could afford to be more selfish. "You let people walk all over you, honey. It's okay to tell people what you want. If you don't, they'll assume what they want is what you want."

Should today be the day I finally take my mom's advice? Should I march up to Xander, pull him away from that woman, and announce to the room that he's mine? Fortunately, Amelia and Noah spot me and wave me over to their table, saving me from embarrassing myself.

Okay, I can see you rolling your eyes at me. Don't

worry, I'd do the same thing in your place. Nobody in their right mind would ever picture me as the type of person who's all, "Sweetheart, get your hands off my man," before planting a big old possessive kiss on my fellow.

"Come sit here, luv." Amelia pats the chair next to her. "We're having some calamari while we wait for the meeting to start. Want some?"

I politely decline her offer. Scary-looking fried tentacles is not my idea of a good meal. "I had some cookies before I came."

"This is exciting, isn't it?" Noah thumps the table, causing one of the tentacles to fly off the plate and into the air. Without blinking an eye, Noah thrusts his knife up, impales the tentacle on it, then tosses the knife back into the air. After catching it with his other hand, Noah casually eats the tentacle directly from the knife. I feel like Noah is the kind of guy you'd want watching your back if you ever find yourself under attack by a gang of jugglers.

After wiping his mouth with a napkin, Noah says, "I was just saying to Amelia that we haven't been involved in a good protest in ages."

Amelia winks at her husband. "Remember the time we dressed up as caterpillars and chained ourselves to the doors of that fast-food restaurant? Such good memories."

"What do caterpillars have to do with fast food?" I

ask.

"That was our strategy." Amelia gives me a knowing smile. "We had the franchise operator so confused about what we were protesting that he decided it would be easier to move the restaurant to another location."

Noah takes a sip of his beer, then asks me, "What about you? What kind of protests have you been involved in?"

"Me? None. Unless you count refusing to go to bed on Christmas Eve. I did that once when I was six." I smile at the thought of my one and only childhood rebellion. See, I can fight for something I want, especially when that something is seeing Santa Claus come down the chimney. Of course, I ended up falling asleep on the couch long before he made an appearance.

Amelia and Noah have an animated discussion about mentoring me in the fine art of protest movements. During the conversation, I learn about techniques to get people to sign petitions, the importance of waterproof markers when lettering slogans on poster board, and the right kind of clothing to wear on marches.

"You'll want comfortable shoes, luv," Amelia says to me. "And wear layers. Sometimes, it can be uncomfortably warm when you're waiting in a holding cell."

My eyebrows shoot up. "Holding cell? You've been

arrested?"

"It comes with the territory," she says as she selects another piece of calamari. "I'll bet the food is good in Greek jails, though."

"Shush, they're starting," Noah says to us.

Here's what Amelia and Noah failed to factor into our involvement in this particular protest meeting—we don't speak Greek. We don't have a clue what's happening.

Admittedly, I'm enjoying watching Xander lead the discussion. He looks so earnest while he's speaking. Gone is the flirtatious joker I've grown accustomed to bantering with. In his place, is a serious man who is determined to save his island from the Humpty Dumpty corporation.

While Xander and others talk about goodness knows what, my mind drifts back to the boomerang incident. It happened during my first assignment as an operations implementation team lead. Humpty Dumpty had just finished construction on a new resort in a remote part of Australia. The hotel rooms and facilities were ready for guests, lush landscaping had been freshly planted, a golf course, tennis courts, and multiple pools had been constructed, and staff members had been hired from the local population.

Training the new staff on the Humpty Dumpty systems and procedures is where I came in. One of my primary duties was to conduct a new employee orientation, or "nesting" in Humpty Dumpty speak.

The fresh hires were required to dress in all white, like an egg, then roll on the floor into a giant nest made out of straw. It was meant to be symbolic—eggs sharing the same nest and all that. In reality, someone always ends up being allergic to the straw the nest is made of and their constant sneezing distracts from the pep talk about our company's values.

I handed a box of tissues to a young woman who couldn't stop sniffling and got the rest of the group's attention. Then I made an exciting announcement. The Chief Rooster was going to join us via video so that he could personally welcome everyone to the Humpty Dumpty flock.

This is where things went wrong. Frank decided to make a surprise appearance—most likely to check up on me—and he burst into the room right as the Chief Rooster was leading the group in the company song.

The poor woman who was having an allergic reaction to the straw sneezed in the middle of the verse about scrambled eggs. This wasn't a dainty sneeze either. The way the building shook, you might have thought we had experienced an earthquake tremor.

There were rumors later at corporate headquarters that shoddy construction might have been to blame for the building shifting the way it did, rather than that woman's sneeze. Regardless, the outcome of the shaking a decorative boomerang hanging on the wall falling onto Frank's head. People laughed when his toupee was knocked off.

Frank's profanity-laced screams caused the building to shake again. Angry and embarrassed, he grabbed the boomerang off the floor and flung it at the sneezing woman.

Here's the thing about boomerangs—sometimes, they tilt in the air, causing them to return to whoever threw them. That's when Frank got hit again, this time in his scrawny chest.

Frank doubled over in pain. I tried to check on him, but he shoved me aside. He stormed over to the sneezing woman and let loose, telling her what a disgrace she was to the company.

She quit on the spot. Can you blame her?

"What an ungrateful clucker," Frank had said as she ran out of the room clutching the box of tissues to her chest. "We don't need their kind in the Humpty Dumpty corporation. Good riddance."

Unfortunately for Frank, the rest of the employees decided to stand in solidarity with her. By the end of the day, we didn't have any staff left, and the resort had to delay its grand opening. Somehow, Frank managed to shift the blame for the walk-out to the recruitment agency, saving his hide in the process.

In a sick sort of way, I admire Frank's ability to weave lies together until you can't remember what the truth was anymore. He wouldn't have had a problem getting anyone to believe he was Canadian or struggle with any moral issues about working on a secret feasibility study.

I startle when I realize Xander is speaking in English. He's pointing at our table and thanking Noah, Amelia, and me for coming and supporting the island in their fight against the Humpty Dumpty corporation.

When the entire room gives us a standing ovation, I want to slide under the table and disappear. Amelia and Noah deserve this acknowledgment. But me? I'm working for the enemy.

After a few more words to the crowd in Greek, the meeting breaks up and Xander comes over to join us. "I can't stay long," he says. "I have to go home and pack."

I frown. "Where are you going?"

"To Athens. I can do more good lobbying on our island's behalf in our capital city. Between Elena and myself, we have contacts with the key stakeholders who can help stop this development."

"Did I hear my name?" I look up and see the woman with long hair and sharp features standing behind Xander. When she places her hands on his shoulders, Xander looks uncomfortable. Or is that my imagination?

After Xander introduces Elena, she expresses her gratitude to us for our involvement. "You can really help with the English social media sites," she says. "In order to be successful, we need to get global attention."

After a tedious discussion about hashtags and selfies, Elena puts her hand in the crook of Xander's arm. "Sorry, I need to steal this one away," she says to us. "Our ferry leaves early in the morning."

I stiffen when I realize she's said, "*our* ferry." They're going to share a ferry. What else do they share? Not that it's any of my business, I remind myself.

Xander seems apologetic as he says goodbye. Or is that my imagination again? Either way, one thing I'm certain of is that he says goodbye to all of us in exactly the same way—a handshake. It's a firm, businesslike handshake. A handshake that lets me know that he's taken me seriously—what happened in the olive grove earlier was a mistake. Now we're friends, nothing more. It makes me feel better about my decision not to divulge who my employer is to Xander.

But, as I watch Xander walk out of the taverna, I can't help wondering why I don't feel better. This is what I wanted, right?

CHAPTER 11
STRONG AND COMPLICATED

It's been a week since Xander left for Athens and three days since I've talked to him. He had called my aunt to check in on the villa and make sure his nephew, Demetrius, was taking care of our needs. When they were done speaking, Aunt Celeste passed the phone to me.

Talk about an awkward conversation. What do you say to someone you made out with in an olive grove? Xander chose a safe subject and asked me about the weather. After telling him that it was still hot and sunny here, I asked if he had seen any donkeys in Athens. When we exhausted those topics, I handed the phone back to my aunt and went into my room to cry.

Sobbing over a man is so pathetic. I hated myself for it. After that crying episode, I vowed never to shed another tear over Xander. So far, I've kept that vow.

Enough dwelling on Xander, I need to focus on the task at hand—getting Midnight out of my suitcase.

"Bad kitty," I say. "I'm leaving in a couple of days. I need to start packing."

The cat yawns in response.

I don't blame him. I'm bored too. Ever since the protest meeting at Athena's taverna, I've been on an actual vacation. Humpty Dumpty's senior management team got wind of how serious the opposition was to building a resort on Gáidaros, and they put the feasibility study on hold. Instead of rejoicing that the immediate threat to the island had diminished, Amelia and Noah seemed disappointed that they didn't have a cause to champion.

Frank was in a vile mood when he called to inform me about the decision to halt the project. "Can you believe those cluckers are scared by a bunch of Greek peasants?" he had said. "I kept telling my colleagues how much money we can make with this resort, but all they can think about is bad PR. Even the Chief Rooster is being a big wuss."

After griping some more about what he would do if he was in charge of the company, Frank said something shocking. "You might as well take time off during the rest of your vacation. Maria is being a real pain in my backside. She's been in the Chief Rooster's office morning, noon, and night lately. Miss High and Mighty is up to something. I don't know what it is yet, but I'll find out. You can count on it. In the meantime, you should lie low."

I'm pretty sure I know what Maria has been discussing with the Chief Rooster, namely the investigation into Frank's conduct. But I kept my mouth shut. The last thing I wanted Frank to know was that I had submitted a report to Maria that didn't exactly cast him in a favorable light.

"Olivia, dear, Demetrius is here," my aunt calls out. "Can you show him the issue we're having with the pool?"

I pick Midnight up out of my suitcase and set him on my bed. He proceeds to hack up a hairball on my pillow as some sort of revenge for not letting him sleep on my clothes. Fine, I'll deal with that later.

When I go out to the patio, Demetrius is watering the plants. When he looks up and smiles at me politely, I'm reminded of his uncle. The two of them share the same dark features and unibrow.

After I show Demetrius the clogged pool filter, he says that he needs to speak with his uncle about getting a part.

"Are you going to call him now?" I ask.

He shakes his head. "I'll speak to him later. I forgot my phone."

"Here, take mine." As I shove my phone into the boy's hand, I realize Xander and I never exchanged phone numbers. Except for that one time we spoke on my aunt's phone, we had only communicated in person. Well, now I'm going to have Xander's number. The question is—what am I going to do with it?

Nothing, Olivia. You're going to do nothing with it, I tell myself firmly.

Demetrius has a brief conversation in Greek, then hands the phone back to me. "My uncle needs to order a part in Athens. He'll bring it back with him."

"When is Xander coming back?"

He shrugs. "Probably not until next week. He's working on something with Elena."

Waves of disappointment wash over me. By the time Xander returns, I'll be gone. Then my disappointment turns into an emotion I'm not proud of—jealousy. I hate that Xander is spending time with Elena instead of me.

When I notice Demetrius wiping sweat off his brow, I offer him something to drink. I grab a couple of sodas out of the fridge, then we sit at the patio table.

"Your uncle said that you spent part of your childhood in the States. That must be why your English is so good."

"I was born in America. I lived there until I was ten."

"Why did you move back to Gáidaros?" I ask.

A shadow passes across the boy's eyes as he takes a sip of his soda. "My mom died, so I came back to live with my grandmother."

My stomach twists in knots. How could I be so

stupid? Xander had hinted at the fact that he had lost his sister. The poor woman died, leaving her son all alone. I want to ask what happened to Demetrius' father, but I don't. I've already opened one wound, one more than I should have.

"I'm so sorry," I say. "I can't imagine what it would be like to lose a parent."

Demetrius nods as he blinks back tears. I want to wrap this boy up in a hug, but I suspect it would help me more than it would help him. Instead, I change the subject. "Your uncle told me you do a good impression of Ned Flanders from *The Simpsons*. Can you show me?"

I spend the next thirty minutes practically peeing my pants because I'm laughing so hard. The kid is amazing. It's uncanny how he can mimic characters' voices and mannerisms.

As I wipe tears of laughter from my eyes, I remember the bet Xander and I had made. "You don't happen to know what your uncle's favorite TV show is by any chance?"

"*Firefly*."

"I've never heard of it."

"It was canceled after one season," Demetrius explains. "It's set in space."

"Well, that explains it. I don't like science fiction."

"But it's also a western, or at least that's what my uncle says."

"That's an odd combination." I wipe a bead of

condensation off my glass before asking. "What is it that he likes about *Firefly*?"

"Don't know. You'll have to ask him." Demetrius finishes his soda, then excuses himself to get back to work.

My phone rings as I'm putting our glasses in the dishwasher. Secretly hoping that it's Xander, I press it against my ear. But instead of hearing Xander's deep voice, I'm greeted by the high-pitched shriek of my old friend, Jasmine.

I've known Jasmine since elementary school. After the Wonder Woman pantsing incident, she stuck by my side, even when the other kids continued to make fun of me. Neither of us is great about staying in touch, but when we do catch up, it's like no time has passed.

"Olivia, you'll never guess who I just saw," she practically yells into the phone. "Do you remember that foreign exchange student during tenth grade? The guy from Denmark."

"Asger?"

"That's it. He's here in Monaco. I ran into him at the Monte Carlo Casino. I barely recognized him. Remember how scrawny he was? Well, not anymore. Muscles everywhere."

As usual, I can't get a word in edgewise. She continues to describe how Asger has turned into a sexy Scandinavian god while I run the dishwasher and wipe down the kitchen counters.

When she pauses to catch a breath, I ask why she's in Monaco. "Is your band on tour there?"

She laughs. "How many times do I have to tell you that it's a string quartet, not a band? We're doing a private concert at some prince's birthday party. Hopefully, he's single."

Now it's my turn to laugh. Jasmine has her heart set on marrying a billionaire. Bonus points if he also happens to be royal. Triple points if he's good-looking.

"A second ago you had your heart set on Asger," I point out.

She scoffs. "He's gorgeous to look at, but the man is a waiter. Anyway, enough about me. I'd ask you about your love life, but I'm sure it will be the same old story. 'I'm too busy with work to date, blah, blah, blah.'"

"Actually, I'm on vacation and I met a guy," I say.

"No way. Where are you?"

"I'm on a beautiful Greek island with my aunt."

"Okay, we'll get back to the island in a minute. First, tell me about this guy."

I spill my guts to Jasmine, telling her about how I met Xander, my involvement in Humpty Dumpty's potential resort on Gáidaros, the investigation into Frank, and Aunt Celeste's insistence that Xander and I are meant for each other.

"Can you believe my aunt thinks love at first sight is a real thing?" I ask.

"She's right," Jasmine says. "You can fall for a guy in less than twenty minutes. Twenty-four hours later, you tell him you love him. Two days after that, you end up getting married."

My eyes widen. "Why do I feel like you're not describing the plot of a Hallmark movie? Did you get married?"

"Kind of yes. But also no. It was annulled, so it's like it never happened." I hear her ask someone for a glass of champagne, then she says to me, "I don't really want to talk about it, if that's okay. Tell me more about your guy. You're obviously smitten with him."

I chuckle. "Smitten? Listen to you. You sound like a character from one of those old movies that my aunt is always watching."

"Smitten is a great word. Don't mock it." Jasmine pretends to be hurt, then says, "Listen, your aunt is right. You definitely have feelings for Xander. And from what you've said, he sounds pretty special. You know how I can tell?"

She pauses to thank someone for her champagne, then says, "All you could talk about was how he makes you laugh. Being able to have fun with someone is the secret to a long-lasting relationship. Of course, they have to have money as well."

"Not only are you a romantic, you're also a cynic," I say.

"I'm realistic. Totally different thing," Jasmine

says. "You said Xander owns lots of property on the island, and he used to be some high-powered corporate type. Sounds like he's loaded. I think you should quit your job and marry him."

Totally ignoring what she said about marriage, I point out, "But I like my job."

"No, you don't," Jasmine says. "You like feeling needed. And Frank manipulates that."

I want to tell her that's not true, but after writing that report for Maria, I'm not so sure. But I'm not ready to admit that to Jasmine. So instead, I deflect. "Humpty Dumpty offers great opportunities for career progression. It's a great company to work for. I'm hoping to get promoted soon."

"I think you should ask yourself why you want a promotion. Is it because you really want a more senior role? Or is it because it would be proof that all the extra hours Frank's manipulated you into working and all the vacation time he's talked you into giving up was worth it?"

Before I can push back, Jasmine tells me she has to go. "Sorry, I have to freshen up before my date. Just think about what I said, okay? Talk soon."

After she hangs up, I set my phone down and rub my temples. I love Jasmine to death, but she has one tiny flaw—she always points out the hard truths and right now I'm not sure I can deal with it.

I decide to go for a walk to clear my head. When I find myself in front of the kafeneio, it brings back memories of when we had coffee there with my aunt. I'm about to push open the door when I hear someone asking if I want to go for a donkey ride.

It sounds like Xander but that doesn't make sense. He's in Athens. I really am getting delusional. Not only can I not stop thinking about Xander, I'm hearing imaginary voices. The lack of sleep is catching up with me. Before I walk inside to order a coffee, someone tugs at my arm.

I spin around and come face-to-face with Xander. Flesh-and-blood Xander, not the Xander that I dreamt about at night. "But, you're in Athens," I splutter. "Demetrius spoke with you earlier."

"I got back earlier today. I told him to pretend I was still in Athens so that I could surprise you." He gives me a cocky grin, then says. "I guess it worked. You look like you're going to faint. Take a seat and I'll get you a coffee. If I remember correctly, you like your coffee strong and bitter."

While I wait for Xander to return, I think about how I like my men, or rather this particular man—strong and complicated. I shake my head, glad Aunt Celeste and Jasmine aren't here. They'd be pushing Xander and me together, and I'm not sure I'd resist.

CHAPTER 12
BURNT BAKLAVA

"Time to get up, sleepyhead," my aunt says the next morning. "Xander will be here soon to give you a cooking lesson."

Turning on my side, I pull the covers over my head. "He's coming this afternoon. I have hours until he gets here," I grumble.

Aunt Celeste yanks the covers off me. I squeeze my eyes shut. Why did she have to open the curtains? Before I can put a pillow over my head, she snatches it away.

"It's almost noon, dear."

I bolt upright. "What? Last time I checked my clock, it was seven."

"You must have needed the sleep," she says.

Rubbing my eyes, I say, "I was tossing and turning all night."

"Thinking about Xander?"

"Yeah. I didn't think I'd see him before I left. Then he shows up and acts like it's no big deal what happened between us."

Aunt Celeste bites back a smile. "You probably want to get your story straight. If I remember correctly, you told me that there wasn't anything going on between you and Xander. Let's see, I think your exact words were, 'Xander and I don't have a future together.'"

I curl up in a ball and pull the covers back over me. "Go away."

She chuckles. "I'll make some coffee while you take a shower. You'll feel more like yourself once you've had some caffeine and done your hair. Then we can have a proper talk about your future."

While I slowly get up, I think about how my parents always joke that Aunt Celeste should have been a professional matchmaker. She loves nothing more than helping people find their perfect romantic partner. Oftentimes, she pairs people who, at first glance, you wouldn't think were compatible, but turn out to be soul mates.

My cousin Shane is a good example. He's a professional football player whose idea of a good time is lifting weights and building model trains. When my aunt introduced him to his now-wife Audra, Shane scoffed. "She's a fashion designer. We don't have anything in common."

Turns out they complement each other perfectly, but they would have never discovered that if Aunt Celeste hadn't intervened. Now they've been married for three years and are expecting their first child.

Lately, I'm beginning to wonder if what my aunt does is more than ordinary matchmaking. Could Aunt Celeste have a little fairy godmother in her? Her instincts are uncanny, almost as though there was some magic at work.

It isn't just my family's romantic relationships she meddles in. My aunt also collects strays who need a little help in the love department. One of them is arriving at the villa later today—a woman named Ginny who Aunt Celeste met on her cruise from Miami to Rome earlier this summer.

Ginny was attending a cooking school in Italy where she met a history professor named Preston. Things were going well until Preston found out she was pretending to be someone she wasn't. Sound familiar?

I guess it gives me some small measure of comfort to know that I'm not the only one who keeps secrets. At least Xander never found out that I work for the Humpty Dumpty corporation. Unlike Ginny, I won't have to deal with the fallout of having my true identity revealed.

Aunt Celeste invited Ginny to come stay with us for a while to get her mind off things. Since my vacation is almost over and I'll be leaving the day after next,

I'm glad Ginny will be here to keep my aunt company. And, more importantly, Aunt Celeste will have someone else to focus her matchmaking on instead of me.

After getting ready, I join my aunt in the kitchen. Midnight is already there, stretched out next to a plate of cookies.

"I went to the bakery this morning to get more melomakarona," Aunt Celeste says. "They're usually only made during the Christmas holidays, but they're available year-round on Gáidaros. Just another reason why this island is so special. Have you ever been to Santa's Village in Finland? They celebrate Christmas all year. Such a fun place."

"The Humpty Dumpty corporation was working on a similar development in Hawaii, but it never got off the ground," I say. "Something about Santa Claus not looking good in shorts."

As I nibble on one of the cookies, my aunt says, "I was surprised you like those, considering they have honey in them."

"I was surprised too." I grin. "The bee vomit seems to be growing on me."

She playfully bats at me with a dish towel. "Don't describe honey like that. It's gross."

"Just calling it what it is."

"Well, if that's the game we're playing, let me call it like I see it. This thing between you and Xander is called"—she pauses for dramatic effect, then says —"Love."

When I nearly snort my coffee out of my nose, Midnight runs over and paws my face.

"Isn't that cute," Aunt Celeste says. "He wants to make sure you're okay."

I pull the cat into my lap, then turn to my aunt. "I haven't known Xander long enough to be in love with him. Instalove is something you read about in romance novels, not something that happens in real life."

"We can't predict love's timing. Sometimes, two people can know each other for years before falling in love. Sometimes, it's instantaneous. Both ways are valid."

"What was it like for you and Uncle Ernie?"

"A little of both," she says wistfully.

Before I can ask her more, Aunt Celeste says she has to check on her crystals. "I'm charging them in the sun so that they'll have more energy. It's helpful to have them fully charged when you're trying to set your intentions."

She offers this up as though it's an explanation, but I don't have a clue what she's talking about. I've never been into all that mystical mumbo-jumbo.

"We should get you a crystal before you leave," she says before she bustles off. "Rose quartz is excellent for opening your heart and cultivating love and forgiveness. I have a feeling that's something you're going to draw on in the future."

* * *

A couple of hours later, I hear Aunt Celeste greeting Xander in an overly loud voice, obviously intending for me to hear. "Olivia has been looking forward to your visit all day. She can't wait to learn how to make baklava."

Xander's voice is so deep that it resonates through the hallway and I don't have to press my ear to the door to hear him. "Are we talking about the same person? Baklava is basically honey layered between sheets of phyllo dough. I thought she hated the stuff."

"She's warming up to honey. Baklava also has nuts," my aunt says. "Olivia likes nuts."

"Maybe there's hope for her taste buds after all," Xander says.

"That's where you come in, dear."

I can't understand what my aunt says next because now she's lowered her voice. It's just like my dad with the remote control—one minute the volume is up, the next minute you need closed captioning to know what's going on.

Worried that Aunt Celeste is having a philosophical discussion with Xander about the merits of love at first sight, I rush out of my room and join them in the kitchen.

"Oh, there you are, dear," my aunt says to me. "I was just talking about you."

I arch an eyebrow. "I'm sure you were."

Xander's back is turned to me, so I can't see his expression. If I had to guess, he has a cocky grin on his face.

When he turns around and hands me a container of walnuts, I realize how wrong I was. He's smiling, but it's not the kinds of smile that reaches his eyes. It reminds me of the first time I left home for college. When my mom dropped me off at my dorm, she gave me one of those bittersweet smiles. She was happy I was starting a new adventure, but sad because she was going to miss me. It was understandable. I felt the same way.

With Xander I'm not quite sure what to make of the mix of emotions I see playing out on his face. I want the cocky, playful Xander back. That guy I understood. This guy confuses me.

Aunt Celeste breaks the silence that's been hanging heavily in the room. "I'll let you two get on with the baklava. I have an appointment at Athena's."

I whip my head around and stare at my aunt. "You're going to see Athena?"

"She invited me for tea. After that, I'm meeting Ginny at the ferry dock." Aunt Celeste glances at her watch. "Gotta go, I don't want to be late."

"What's that about?" I ask Xander after she leaves.

"Honestly, I'm a little worried." Xander rubs his

chin. "If the two of them decide to put what happened behind them and join forces, they would be a pretty scary duo."

"I still don't know what happened," I say. "Every time I ask my aunt, she makes up an excuse not to talk about it."

"Maybe she's embarrassed about it. It was a stupid misunderstanding that blew up into something more." Xander shrugs. "That's what happens when both people have big personalities." He claps his hands together. "Well, should we get on with this cooking lesson?"

Xander smiles as he hands me an apron. This time it's an ordinary smile, one you'd give to an acquaintance who you run into on the street. But I know the truth. He's good at hiding what he feels, just like I am.

We start off making phyllo dough from scratch. I could have sworn they sold this stuff already made that you can buy frozen, but apparently that isn't an option for Xander. It takes us a few hours—partly because Midnight decided to jump into a bowl of flour at one point and we had to start over.

By the time we're ready to assemble the baklava, we've slipped back into a mild form of hate-flirting. There's an undercurrent there, but it's tempered by something. Fear, maybe?

"Baklava usually has thirty-three layers of phyllo dough," Xander says as he melts butter. "Did you know phyllo was first mentioned in Homer's Odyssey?"

"My, aren't you a fountain of information?"

Xander chuckles. "Why don't you mix the nuts with the cinnamon and cloves while I make the syrup?"

"Come and meet my niece," I hear my aunt say in the hallway.

I turn to greet the auburn-haired woman poking her head into the kitchen. "You must be Ginny," I say. "I'm Olivia, and this is my friend, Xander."

Xander gives a casual wave with the spatula in his hand, then scoops honey out of the jar into a bowl.

"You're just in time," I say. "He's going to teach us how to make baklava."

Aunt Celeste shakes her head as she surveys the kitchen—things have gotten a bit chaotic since she left. Then she points to Xander, saying, "He owns the taverna by the ferry dock. You must have seen it when you arrived. It's just up the hill."

I shoot my aunt a look. Did she just say that Xander owns the taverna? Why is it called Athena's? What's the connection? Realizing that now isn't the time to get into that, I say to Ginny, "We ate dinner there when I first arrived. Xander is the best cook on the island."

Xander sets the spatula and honey on the counter, then brushes a lock of hair off my face. "I think you might be a bit biased."

I startle at the unexpected display of intimacy. Is this a show for my aunt and Ginny? I have a lot of questions for Xander once we're alone. Two can play this game, though. I smile brightly at Xander. "Not at all. I know what I like and I like your cooking."

When my aunt clears her throat, I realize Xander and I have been staring into each other's eyes. "I'm going to show Ginny to her room," she says. "Be sure to save some of that baklava for us."

Once they leave, I pull back and cross my arms over my chest. "What was that about?"

"I didn't like the way you referred to me as a 'friend' when you introduced me to Ginny," Xander says grumpily.

I press my lips together. "But isn't that what we are? Friends? We agreed that what happened in the olive grove was a mistake."

"We did," Xander concedes. "But it doesn't mean I have to like it."

My shoulders slump. "I don't like it either, but I'm leaving tomorrow to go back to my normal life."

"I know," he says quietly before kissing me on my forehead. Then he pulls away, and we finish assembling the baklava in silence.

While we're sitting at the kitchen table waiting for the baklava to bake, I ask Xander about what my aunt said earlier. "I didn't realize you owned the taverna."

He cocks his head to one side. "You didn't?"

"No, not at all," I say. "But now that I know, I guess

it makes more sense that you cooked spanakopita there for me."

"Which you never ate," Xander points out. "I can't believe you told Ginny you like my cooking when you've never tried it."

"I'm about to," I say, pointing at the oven. "But back to the taverna. If you own it, why is it called Athena's?"

He wrinkles his brow. "Because she's my—"

Before he can finish his sentence, Athena herself barges into the kitchen.

"When Celeste told me what was happening, I had to see for myself," she says, her eyes wild. She slaps Xander on the back of his head, then turns to me. "I'm sorry if my son has been leading you on, but there can never be a future between the two of you.

"Your son?" My eyes dart back and forth between the two of them before landing on Xander. "She's your mother?"

Xander holds his hands up. "I thought you knew that."

Athena speaks in rapid-fire Greek to Xander. Their discussion gets louder and louder, and I'm sure even people on Rhodes can hear what they're saying. After a while, Athena gives Xander a triumphant grin, then marches out of the kitchen.

"What was that about?" I ask.

Xander takes a deep breath, then rests his hand on my arm. "We're just friends, right?"

"Yeah." I fidget with the tablecloth while I wait for him to continue.

"Well, I agreed to get fixed up on three dates with, um, three different . . ."

I watch as Xander tries to find the words, then I decide to put him out of his misery. "Your mom is playing matchmaker. She wants you to fall in love with a nice Greek girl. Not someone inappropriate like me. It'll be like a game show. You'll get three chances to find the perfect girl. Well, perfect for your mom, at least."

As he nods, the oven timer goes off. When I pull the tray of baklava out, I notice that it's burned on top. You couldn't get a clearer message from the universe than this.

CHAPTER 13
THE GODDESS OF SPRING

Xander tries to scrape the burnt layers off the baklava, but it's no use. It's charred all the way through. After he dumps it in the trash, I suggest we have a drink.

"Why don't you make more of that soumada for us?"

Xander hesitates. "It's late. Don't you think I should get going?"

"I don't want you to go yet." I set the baklava pan in the sink to soak, then turn back to Xander. "After what happened with your mother, I need to decompress."

"Yeah, me too," he says as he wipes crumbs off the counter. "I can't believe I agreed to go out on these dates."

"I guess you're a mama's boy."

"It's not that. Believe me, I don't normally do everything she wants." Xander's jaw tightens. "But after what happened with my sister . . ."

"If you don't want to talk about it, I understand."

Xander tosses the sponge in the sink. "Come on, let's get that soumada."

I follow Xander to the outdoor kitchen area. As he makes our drinks, I'm reminded of the first day we met. Xander had been so light-hearted at the time, joking and flirting with me. Now, he's a shadow of himself. I want to hold him in my arms and take away some of his pain, but I sense that he's the type of man who needs distance when he's hurting.

As Xander hands me my glass, he gives me a brittle smile. "We traditionally drink soumada on happy occasions, like weddings or baptisms."

"Why don't we have something else?"

He shakes his head. "It seems appropriate somehow. My sister loved soumada."

"What was her name?"

"Persephone."

"She was the goddess of spring, wasn't she?"

Xander arches an eyebrow. "I'm surprised you know that."

"I had a book on Greek mythology when I was younger. I always liked the story of Persephone."

"It's a story of a mother's love for her child," Xander says. "Because Persephone ate pomegranate seeds, she was forced to spend four months each year in the underworld with Hades. Persephone's mother, Demeter, would be so distraught at the loss of her daughter that the plants would wither and die."

"Her sadness caused fall and winter to happen, right?"

Xander bites back a smile. I have a feeling he was about to come back with a snappy retort. But then sadness quickly washes over his face. "When Persephone's time in the underworld was over each year, she'd return to her mother. Demeter would be so happy at being reunited with her daughter that the plants would grow and the flowers would blossom."

"The promise of spring," I say softly.

"Exactly," Xander says. "Spring always returns. It's hard for my mother to see that right now. She lost hope when my sister died. Then, when my father passed away not long after from a heart attack, she sank into a deep despair. All that's left now is bitterness."

I take a chance, sliding my hand across the bar and gently squeezing his. He tenses. I think he's going to pull away, but instead he lifts my hand to his lips and lightly kisses the back of it. Then he raises his glass. "To Persephone."

I clink my glass with his, joining in with the toast to his sister. We sit quietly, watching the sunset while we sip our soumada. As the darkness envelops us, Xander tells me more about his family.

"My father was a doctor. He was offered a job at a

hospital in Texas, and we moved there when I was just a baby. Persephone hadn't been born yet—she was three years younger than me."

"But how come you don't have a Texan accent like your mother?"

"It sounds funny when she says 'y'all,' doesn't it? Sometimes, I think she deliberately lays it on thick for effect." Xander chuckles, then says, "After I graduated high school, I went to college in New York, then got my MBA at Harvard. I'm one of those people who picks up the accent of places where I'm living. I end up mimicking the people I'm around unintentionally."

"Me, too," I say. "My last assignment was in Toronto. I started to sound like a Canadian."

"Celeste says you've worked all over the world. I guess that's something we have in common."

I stiffen, afraid he's going to ask me who my employer is. Instead, he continues to tell me about his family's history. "My sister stayed in Texas after high school. She got mixed up with a bad crowd and dropped out of college. When she got pregnant, my parents were horrified that she refused to marry the father. It was probably for the best. The guy ended up skipping town."

"Wasn't he a part of Demetrius' life?" I ask.

"No, my sister was a single mom. I was in awe of how she juggled everything. She got a decent job and even went back to school at night to get her college degree. Everything was going great."

"Then what happened?"

"Demetrius' father turned back up. He had been in and out of prison by this point, but Persephone still couldn't see straight when it came to that guy. He would snap his fingers and she'd come running."

It's hard to see Xander's expression in the faint moonlight, but I could swear his eyes are glistening. He turns away to make us more soumada before I can be sure.

"Here you go," Xander says, his voice cracking slightly as he hands me my glass.

We make another toast to his sister, then he says, "Persephone went out to a bar with him one night. They both had way too much to drink, but that—"

Xander clenches his fist and mutters something in Greek. "Sorry," he says. "Anyway, he and another guy decided to drag race. My sister tried to talk him out of it, but he wouldn't listen. He told Persephone that if she loved him, she'd get in the passenger seat."

"My sister got in the car." Xander pauses for a moment to rub his eyes. "He started the engine, they got up to speed, then he swerved to avoid something on the road. The car flipped over. They both died at the scene."

Xander might be holding back his tears, but mine come rushing out. I can't imagine living with a tragedy like this. No wonder Athena is so bitter. No wonder she's lost hope. I get up and grab a napkin to dab my eyes.

"Hey, it's okay," Xander says as he pulls me into an embrace.

I sniffle. "I'm the one who should be comforting you."

"You are." He strokes my hair. "I don't know why it's so easy to tell you about what happened to Persephone. I've never really talked about it before. Honestly, I never feel like it's my story to tell since it happened to her."

"I'm your friend," I say. "No matter what happens, remember that."

"It's more than that," he says. "I have other friends, but none of them are quite like you."

I take a step back before I move us out of the friend zone by kissing him. Xander seems to understand because he moves back around to the other side of the bar, putting some much needed space between us.

"My mother is very traditional," Xander says. "Growing up, we tended to socialize with folks from the Greek community in our part of Texas. There was an assumption that my sister would marry a nice Greek boy. A guy from Greece would have been great, but a Greek-American would have been fine as well. What my mother didn't expect was for my sister to fall for someone who came from a completely different background."

Midnight jumps onto the bar, interrupting Xander for a moment. Once the cat decides where the best place to lie down is—apparently it's right next to me so that I can pet him—Xander continues. "It might have been okay if he showed some interest in learning about Greek culture, but all the guy wanted to do was watch football and drink."

"Football is big in Texas," I say.

"I was the quarterback on my high school football team," Xander says with a bit of pride in his voice. "And my dad and I used to watch football games together. There were lots of American traditions and pastimes that we adopted as a family. But we were also proud of our Greek heritage, and when that guy didn't care enough about my sister to want to learn about any of it, well, that should have been a big clue. I just wish Persephone had seen him for what he was before she got pregnant."

"But then she wouldn't have had Demetrius," I say. "He seems like a pretty special kid."

Xander nods. "You're right. I'm glad I left my corporate job and moved back to Gáidaros so that I can spend more time with him."

"Why did you leave corporate life?" I ask.

"When my uncle passed away, he didn't have any children, so I inherited his property. By this point, my mother and Demetrius had already moved back here. She couldn't bear to stay in the States after losing Persephone and my dad. One day, as I was walking through the olive grove, it hit me. Everything that's important to me is on this island. So I quit."

"You make it sound so simple."

"The right decisions often are the simplest ones."

As I stroke Midnight, something dawns on me. "That's why your mother wants you to settle down with a Greek girl. She's worried the same thing will happen to you that happened to your sister."

"I've told her a million times how irrational it is, but she's not ready to accept that." Xander lets out a long sigh. "There are a few universal truths, no matter what your nationality or cultural background is. Heartbreak is one of them."

"There's another universal truth," I say. "You can find love where you least expect it."

Xander looks at me sharply, and I shake my head.

"What I mean is that you should give these Greek girls your mother is going to fix you up with a chance. One of them might be perfect for you. And, if you marrying a Greek woman gives your mother some measure of comfort, well then, all the better."

Xander considers this for a moment, then says softly, "You really are a good friend."

"To friends," I say as I raise my glass.

After we finish our soumada, Xander says, "What time are you leaving tomorrow?"

"I'm taking the afternoon ferry," I say.

"Okay," he says. "I'll come by in the morning to say goodbye."

As he kisses me lightly on the cheek, I fight back tears again. This time, they're for me. Our heart-to-heart tonight has made me realize the depth of my feelings for Xander. Can I really get on the ferry tomorrow knowing I'll be saying goodbye to him forever?

* * *

As I'm packing the next morning, Maria calls me. After exchanging a few pleasantries, she asks, "Why didn't you tell me you were spending your vacation on Gáidaros?"

The muscles in my shoulders tense. I think I know what's coming. "Um, I guess it never came up."

Maria sighs. "I wish you had told me. Then I could have prevented what happened. Frank should have never called you and asked you to work on the feasibility study. You were supposed to be on vacation."

"I'm so sorry," I say, cringing as I hear how squeaky my voice sounds. I bite my lower lip while I wait for Maria to fire me. She had warned me that if I didn't take vacation, there would be consequences. I'm prepared to face them.

Much to my surprise, Maria says, "Don't worry, you're not in trouble. Frank manipulated you into working on the project. It's not your fault."

It would be easy to let her assume that was the whole story, but the truth of the matter is that I wanted to work on the project. I had seen it as a ticket to advancement in the company. My talk with Jasmine had made me realize why I wanted to be promoted—it would have validated all my long hours at work and my complete lack of a personal life. But that doesn't negate the fact that I willingly agreed to Frank's request.

When I tell Maria all this, I feel like a weight has been lifted off my shoulders. It's like my mom always says, "Telling the truth doesn't cost you anything, but not telling it can cost you everything."

"I blame myself, really," Maria says. "I should have intervened earlier. Frank has no business managing people. True leaders nurture their employees' natural gifts. Frank just twists them for his own purposes."

She sighs. "Did you know he actually told everyone on the senior management team that he was personally carrying out the feasibility study? We all assumed he was on Gáidaros when he video conferenced into meetings. But no, he was sitting back, taking credit for your hard work."

"Where was he?" I ask.

"He was in Tahiti." Maria snorts. "On vacation. Can you believe it?"

Maria vents about Frank for a few more minutes, then turns the conversation back to me.

"Listen, here's what I want you to do. I want you to take two actual weeks of vacation. It doesn't matter where you spend them, just take time off for yourself. Take the opportunity to really reflect on what you want out of life, personally and career-wise. I'll support you no matter what you decide is the right path forward for you." I hear her typing on her computer, then she says. "I think you could benefit from some coaching. The company is going to pay for it. I've emailed the details of a woman who I think would be a good fit for you. She does virtual sessions, so if you want to start working with her now, you can."

I furrow my brow. This was not the outcome I expected. At the beginning of this conversation, I thought I was going to be fired. Now, I'm being offered career coaching. I'm at a loss for words, so I say the first stupid thing that comes to mind. "You cut off my access to the company servers."

Maria laughs. "I've restored your access, so you'll be able to get the email I sent you." Then she says in a more serious tone, "Frank has been put on a temporary leave of absence pending the outcome of our investigation. So you don't have to worry about him calling you and pressuring you to work."

"He probably wasn't happy about that," I say.

"That's an understatement," Maria says. "Now, where are you going to spend your vacation? I imagine you'll want to get as far away from Gáidaros as possible."

"I'm not sure," I tell Maria, but as I utter those words, I realize it's not true. I know exactly where I'm going to spend the next two weeks—here on Gáidaros.

CHAPTER 14
YODELING BRINGS
PEOPLE TOGETHER

After deciding to stay on Gáidaros for my new, real vacation, I fell into a comfortable routine. In the mornings, after a leisurely breakfast with my aunt—and Ginny when we could get her to come out of her room—I would go for a long walk and explore the island. I was starting to wear out my Converse sneakers with all the miles I had been putting on them.

After a simple lunch of fruit and yogurt, I would read by the pool or dabble in watercolor painting with my aunt. Then Xander would join us for happy hour. Aunt Celeste shared stories that would have us rolling on the ground with laughter, Xander told us about Greek history and culture, and I read poetry out loud.

Yes, you heard that right—poetry. A previous guest

had left several poetry books at the villa. In the past, I would have skipped right over them, but now, taking the time to read a poem slowly and savor each word appeals to me now. My internal rhythm has shifted somehow, adapting to the slow pace of life on Gáidaros. I'm not sure how I'm going to go back to the fast-paced, high pressure world of work.

After happy hour, Xander would take off. By some sort of unspoken agreement, we didn't talk about what his plans were after he left the villa. The last thing I wanted to know was if he had a date planned.

Now, as I'm getting toward the end of my first week of real vacation, I make a crazy suggestion to my aunt while we're putting our painting supplies away. "What do you think about me cooking Xander and his mother dinner tonight?"

She laughs. "Which of your specialties are you going to make? Grilled cheese or pancakes?"

"Very funny," I say. "Actually, I was thinking of cooking Greek food."

"Greek food? You?"

"Come on, you have to admit that I've become more adventurous in eating. I tried that eggplant you made last night."

"That's true. And you didn't spit it out in your napkin when you thought I wasn't looking." Aunt Celeste smiles. "Vacation seems to be doing you good."

"Spending time with you is doing me good." I

squeeze my aunt's hand before going to grab a cookbook from the kitchen. When I rejoin her on the patio, I ask, "What do you think I should make?"

"Let's see, it should be something simple." She flips through the pages, then points at a recipe. "How about souvlaki? It's cubes of meat that you marinate, then grill on a skewer. You could serve it with some potatoes cooked with lemon and oregano."

"That sounds good," I say.

While I examine the recipe, my aunt asks, "Are you sure you want to do this? Athena runs a restaurant and Xander prides himself on his cooking."

"It's making an effort that counts," I say. "I want to demonstrate that I'm taking an interest in Greek culture and food."

"It's a sweet gesture," she says. "But I have to ask, who is it you're trying to impress—Athena or Xander? Because if it's Xander, then why? You're just friends, right? And if it's his mother, then that's an even bigger why."

"It's just dinner," I snap.

"If you say so, dear."

I rub my temples, feeling a headache coming on for the first time this week. "I'm sorry. I know you're only trying to help."

"It's okay." My aunt gives me a sympathetic smile. "I shouldn't meddle, but I think there's something you should know about Xander and his family."

I lean forward. "What is it?"

"I know I tried to push you and Xander together at first, but I think that was a mistake."

"You do?" I feel crestfallen. Part of me has been harboring a secret hope that somehow Xander and I would end up together. But knowing my aunt thinks Xander and I don't belong together makes me realize what a stupid fantasy that is.

"In another world, in another time, you two would be perfect for each other. But after Athena and I had a heart-to-heart over tea, I've come to understand her better." Aunt Celeste twists her wedding ring on her finger while she stares off into the distance. "You see, Athena had a daughter—"

"Is this about Persephone being killed in a car accident?" I blurt out.

My aunt's eyes widen. "You knew about that?"

"Xander and I had our own heart-to-heart. He told me all about it."

"Well, then you understand why Athena is so controlling of her son's love life." She shakes her head. "Maybe in time Athena will soften, but right now Xander would have to make a choice between you and his mother."

"I would never feel right if he chose me over her." I take a deep breath, then smile brightly. "So don't worry, this dinner is just a dinner. Okay?"

"Agreed," my aunt says as she jokingly shakes my hand. Then she says in a more serious tone, "I feel so sorry for Athena. I wish I had known about her daughter before I put my foot in it."

I give her a sympathetic look. "What exactly happened?"

"Well, it was the day I arrived on Gáidaros. I went to the taverna for dinner and got to chatting with Athena. You know what I'm like. I started telling her silly stories about my life. Unfortunately, one of them was about drag racing."

I put my hand to my mouth. "Oh, no."

"Athena flew into a rage. A totally understandable reaction given Persephone's tragic accident." Aunt Celeste blinks back a tear. "But at the time, I didn't know what had happened to the poor girl, so I let Athena have it back. Which I shouldn't have done. I should have risen above it. Instead, I behaved childishly."

"That's why you were so evasive whenever I asked you about it," I say.

"It was so embarrassing." My aunt wrings her hands. "Two widows fighting like that in front of everyone."

"I get that," I say. "We've all done things we're not proud of."

"Xander was so sweet," my aunt says. "He got his mother to calm down, then escorted me back to the villa."

"He didn't tell you about his sister, then?"

"No, and I understand that. It can't be easy for him to talk about it. Xander was very reassuring. He told me not to worry about his mother, that it would all blow over," she says. "Xander was right. Athena eventually told me about Persephone and we made peace. I actually think it helped her in some small way to talk about it with someone other than a family member."

"Maybe we should make dinner for Xander and Athena together?" I suggest. "Athena might appreciate that."

"That would be lovely, dear," my aunt says. "Why don't I make dessert?"

"Sounds good, as long as it's not burnt baklava."

* * *

"What are you thinking about, dear?" my aunt asks as we wait in the living room for Ginny.

"How horribly things went last night," I say. "The dinner I made for Athena and Xander was a disaster on every level."

Aunt Celeste shakes her head. "That's not true."

"How can you say that?" I scoff. "The grill caught on fire. I put sugar on the potatoes instead of salt. Midnight hacked up a hairball on Athena's chair. The only redeeming feature of the night was your dessert. Thank goodness you made plenty of it because it was the only edible thing on the table."

"I enjoyed your souvlaki," she says.

"You tried to feed it to the cat. And even he

wouldn't eat it." I chuckle. "Did you notice how Athena kept a close eye on Xander and me? Whenever she thought we might be overstepping the line between friends and more-than-friends, she'd tell us about the girls she had lined up for Xander to date. I thought there were only supposed to be three dates. It seems like she's organized way more than that."

My aunt gives me a sympathetic smile. "That must have been hard to listen to."

"Actually, I was glad when she did that. It reminded me that Xander is off limits." I glance at the clock on the wall and wonder what's keeping Ginny. "It was nice to see how well you and Athena got along."

"We really do have a lot in common," my aunt says. "Can you believe we both learned how to yodel after seeing a Swiss Miss commercial?"

"Where is Ginny?" I ask, rubbing my stomach. "I'm starved."

Aunt Celeste grins. "I can't believe you're actually going to try Xander's moussaka tonight."

"It's just to shut him up," I joke." He's been complaining about the fact that I've never tried his cooking."

"Oh, here she is." My aunt smiles at Ginny when she walks into the living room. "You look lovely, dear."

"That color really suits you," I say. "And the way the straps cross in the back is super cute."

"Thanks," Ginny says as she smooths down the front of her dress. "Sorry, I've been such a terrible house guest. You must think that I'm pathetic, the way I've been holed up in my room crying my eyes out over a guy."

"Trust me, dear," my aunt says. "It will all work itself out. The universe has your best interests at heart. That reminds me. I have something for both of you."

Ginny and I exchange glances when Aunt Celeste hands each of us a small velvet pouch. "Inside is a crystal that I picked out specifically for each of you," she says.

"What is it?" Ginny holds up a pearlescent white stone.

"It's a moonstone," my aunt tells her. "It has protective powers. Plus, if you put it underneath your pillow at night, it will help you sleep."

"I could use a good night's sleep," Ginny says.

Aunt Celeste smiles at her, then turns to me. "I chose rose quartz for you. It's wonderful for opening one's heart to love and forgiveness."

"It's very pretty," I say. "But I've come to terms with the fact that Xander and I will only ever be friends."

"Don't worry." My aunt gives me a cryptic smile. "I also gave a rose quartz to Xander. There may be a time in the future when he needs it."

"What does that mean?" I ask.

Ignoring my question, Aunt Celeste claps her hands together. "Come on, girls. We don't want to be late."

Xander's dinner is absolutely delicious. I'm proud of myself for not having to close my eyes to eat the moussaka. I look it straight in the face—not that eggplant casseroles have faces, but you get what I mean—stick my fork in it, and scoop the gooey goodness into my mouth without hesitation.

Ginny must love it too, based on the way she's scarfing it down. While she asks for seconds, I excuse myself and go to the ladies' room. Washing my hands feels a bit nostalgic. It's hard to believe that the last time I was in here, I was sobbing my eyes out over Xander. The girl looking back at me in the mirror surprises me—her eyes are sparkling, she looks confident, and she seems happy. She sure has changed since arriving on this island, and it's a change for the better.

When I return to the table, I notice Xander and Ginny whispering to each other. Before I can find out what they're conspiring about, Xander asks who wants baklava. Everyone raises their hands, including me.

After dessert—and, by the way, baklava that isn't burnt within an inch of its life is delicious—Xander tells us he has a surprise for us. He summons Demetrius over. After introducing his nephew to Ginny, he nudges him. "Go on."

Demetrius shyly hands each of us a bracelet.

"My nephew made these," Xander says proudly. He points at the blue and white charm dangling from the bracelets. "That's an evil eye. It will protect you from harm."

My aunt whispers to me, "A crystal and an evil eye in one day. The universe must really be looking out for you."

Athena joins us while we have coffee. While she and my aunt chat about yodeling techniques, Xander motions for me to join him on the terrace.

"Dinner was delicious," I say. "Much better than last night."

"Don't be so hard on yourself," he says. "That was the first time you tried cooking Greek food."

I sigh. "And the last."

"When you fall down, you have to get back up on the donkey."

"I think you mean horse, but I take your point."

Xander smiles. "I have an idea. Why don't we try cooking together? There's a dish my mother loves and I know she'd be thrilled if we made it for her."

"I'm not sure that's a good idea." I look back at the table. Athena seems in good spirits now, but what will she think if Xander and I spend time in the kitchen cooking together? She'll probably want to chaperon us.

"Trust me," Xander says. "What could possibly go wrong?"

CHAPTER 15
AN UNEXPECTED VISITOR

A week later, my aunt and I are sitting on the patio waiting for Xander to arrive for happy hour. It's just the two of now that Ginny has returned to the States. Actually, make that three. Midnight never lets us forget that he's the prime resident of this villa.

"I can't believe it's your last day of vacation," my aunt says. "How are you feeling about it?"

"Strange," I say. "When Maria said that I had to take time off, I initially fought it."

Aunt Celeste snorts. "You did more than fight it. You worked while you were supposed to be on vacation."

"I realize now what a big mistake that was on so many levels," I say. "When Maria gave me another chance to take a real vacation, it took me a while to get in the groove of relaxing. But disconnecting and relaxing for these past two weeks was exactly what I needed."

"Sounds like you're now an official member of Team Vacation," my aunt says. "It sure beats Team Workaholic, doesn't it?"

"Yes, but I am looking forward to getting back to work tomorrow. I don't think I could ever be on permanent vacation."

"You might change your tune when you get closer to retirement age. But you're a long way away from that." My aunt wipes down the patio table, then asks, "Tell me more about your new job."

"It's not really a new job," I say. "It's just a temporary assignment because the investigation into Frank is still ongoing."

Aunt Celeste motions for me to help put the tablecloth on, then says, "Why is it taking so long?"

"I think there are lawyers involved." I straighten out my side of the tablecloth, then add, "Anyway, Maria's arranged for me to work on a special project for the time being. It's actually really interesting. Humpty Dumpty is doing a strategic review of their value proposition, in particular looking at the quantified value of their products and differentiation from their competitors."

"Do you mind translating that word salad you just spit out?"

I grin. "Basically, they're trying to decide if they should overhaul their resort business."

"Well, something needs fixing. Otherwise, Humpty Dumpty is going to have a great fall," my aunt says. "How long are you going to be working on this project?"

I shrug. "I don't know. Things are kind of fluid right now. I'm just happy that I can work remotely."

"I'm glad you decided to work remotely from here for the next few weeks," Aunt Celeste says. "I've really enjoyed spending this time with you."

I wag a finger at her. "But starting tomorrow, I have to work. I can't lounge by the pool or do watercolor painting."

"That's just during the day. During the evenings and on weekends, you can hang out with me and Xander." She smiles. "It's great how the two of you have become such good friends. I imagine that it hasn't been easy."

"It wasn't at first, but we've made it work. As long as he doesn't talk about the women he's dating, we're good." I shake my head. "Athena still sees me as a threat, though. Every time I'm at the taverna, she brings a new girl over to introduce to Xander. Right in front of me. There aren't that many people on the island. Where does she keep finding them?"

"Give her time," my aunt says.

"Time I can give her," I say. "Just not any more dinners. That's two times I've cooked for her and each time was a disaster. The first time, I understand. After all, I did set the grill on fire. But the second time,

Xander helped me cook, and we made her favorite dish. She could have smiled once during the meal. Instead, all she did was complain that the food was giving her a tummy ache."

"It wasn't your food," Aunt Celeste says. "There was a stomach bug going around. I'm sure she realized that later."

"I know I should be more patient with her, but she doesn't make it easy," I say. "Anyway, speaking of food, I'm going to get the appetizers."

While I'm arranging cheese and olives on a platter, my aunt pokes her head in the kitchen.

"Olivia, there's someone here to see you." She wrings her hands together. "I think you should get out there."

I rush outside and see my boss pacing back and forth. Frank is wearing his usual three-piece pinstripe suit, but he's paired it with a bucket hat and flip-flops. This must be his version of business casual dress.

"What are you doing here?" I ask, bracing myself for a confrontation.

Frank narrows his eyes and utters a string of profanities. "It was you, wasn't it? You're the reason why I was fired."

My eyes widen. "You were fired?"

"Don't play dumb." He presses his thin lips together. "You and that witch Maria conspired against me."

I hold up my hands. "There wasn't any conspiracy."

"You couldn't keep your mouth shut about what happened in Australia, could you?" Frank clenches his fists. "If you remember, I was the one who was injured by the boomerang. I had a black eye for weeks. The company should be compensating me, not that sniveling woman and all those other ungrateful people."

"You had it coming, Frank," I say. "I regret not speaking up before now."

My boss—correction, former boss—looks around the courtyard with wild eyes before grabbing a flower pot. He flings it in my direction. I duck just in time and it smashes into pieces against a wall.

As I crouch down to shield myself from further attacks, I hear someone shriek. At first, I think it's me, but then I realize it's coming from Frank. Midnight has sunk his claws into Frank's leg. He must have scratched him good because I can see blood dripping down onto Frank's sandals. Frank swings his leg back and forth to try to get the cat off, but Midnight clings on for dear life.

The gate to the courtyard creaks open and I hear a familiar voice bellow, "What's going on here?"

I look up, relieved to see Xander. Midnight seems to take Xander's arrival as a sign that his work here is done. He lets go of Frank's leg, casually pads over to one of the lounge chairs, then calmly washes behind his ears.

Xander rushes over and helps me to my feet. "Olivia, are you okay?"

"I'm fine," I say as I brush a few shards of broken pottery off my pants.

After checking to make sure I'm not injured, Xander storms over to Frank and grabs him by his lapels. "Want to tell me what's going on here, buddy?"

"Nothing," Frank says without his usual bluster. "It's a silly misunderstanding."

"You threw a flowerpot at me," I say.

"Doesn't sound like a misunderstanding." Xander's voice might sound calm, but there's a steely undercurrent leaving no doubt that he's restraining his fury.

Frank starts to say something, but Xander shushes him. Then he points at a patio chair, commanding Frank to sit. I give a silent cheer when Frank obeys.

I hear someone behind me and turn around. Aunt Celeste is standing by the doorway, her hands over her mouth. After a moment, she points at Frank. "Is that your boss?"

"My former boss," I say. "He was fired."

"I knew it was a mistake to assign you to the feasibility study," Frank says to me. "You never had what it took to work for the Humpty Dumpty corporation. I should have never hired you in the first place."

When I realize that the truth I've been hiding from Xander has finally come out, I feel the blood draining from my face. I can't bear to face at Xander, but he doesn't give me a choice. He walks over to me and lifts my chin with his finger, forcing me to look him in the eyes.

"Is this true, Olivia?" His voice is icy. It sends chills down my spine. "Were you Humpty Dumpty's spy on Gáidaros? Did you lie to me this whole time?"

I want to deny it, but I can't hide from the truth any longer. "Yes, it's all true. I'd tell you how sorry I was for what I've done, but I know it won't make a difference."

He holds my gaze for a moment longer before saying, "Finally, she speaks the truth. You're right. Nothing you could ever say would make the slightest difference."

As he walks out of the courtyard and out of my life forever, tears flow down my face. When Aunt Celeste pulls me into an embrace, I whisper, "I can't stay on Gáidaros. I need to get away from here."

"I have an idea," Aunt Celeste says. "How about if we go on a Rhine riverboat cruise?"

I wipe my eyes. What a totally random suggestion, but I'll do anything to get off this island. "Sure. Let's pack our bags."

* * *

A few days later, my aunt and I are making our way up the gangway to our riverboat, the Abenteuer. We'll spend the next ten days cruising from Amsterdam in the Netherlands, down the Rhine River, before disembarking in Basel, Switzerland. I can't believe that I get to go on this trip, let alone be paid to do so.

After Frank showed up on Gáidaros and destroyed my life, all I could think about was getting away. When Aunt Celeste suggested this Rhine River cruise, I eagerly agreed. Then I called Maria and told her about the altercation with Frank. She was horrified. After assuring me that Humpty Dumpty's lawyers would make sure Frank never bothered me again, I broached the subject of taking some unpaid leave so that I could go on the cruise with my aunt. To my surprise, Maria told me that the company is in confidential merger discussions with the company that owns the riverboat cruise line.

"Consider it a working vacation," she said. "Make notes about the cruise from your perspective as a passenger. Then submit a report when it's over."

"It sounds like you want me to be a spy," I said.

"No, not at all," she reassured me. "We've discussed the idea with our potential partners. You'll be like a mystery shopper in a store. You can tell us what works well on the cruise, and what areas could use improvement."

As I walk aboard the boat, I instantly know one of the things I'm going to include in my report—how exciting it is to be experiencing something that isn't American-centric. Everyone around me is speaking different languages and there are small flags from around the world hanging from the ceiling.

As I'm trying to figure out which country the flag with the parrot on it belongs to, my aunt nudges me. She points at one of the women behind the reception desk. "See the tall girl there? That's Isabelle. I can't figure out why she's wearing her hair in that horrible bun. It doesn't suit her."

"It could be a dress code requirement," I say.

Isabelle startles when she sees us. "Celeste? I thought you were in Greece," she says.

Aunt Celeste rushes over and envelops Isabelle in a hug. "Surprise."

"Remember how I was telling you I won tickets for a transatlantic cruise? That's how my friend Mia and I got to Europe," Isabelle says to her colleague. "Well, that's when I met Celeste. She kind of adopted us, along with Ginny, this other girl we met on board."

"I like to think of myself as you girls' fairy godmother. Whenever one of you has troubles with your love life, I'm there to help out." Aunt Celeste pinches Isabelle's cheeks, then says, "Now, come meet my niece, Olivia. She's been staying with me in Greece."

While I'm shaking Isabelle's hand, my aunt says,

"Olivia met a wonderful guy—he owns a taverna near my villa. He makes the most divine baklava. But his mother . . . well, let's just say that I thought it would be good for Olivia to get away for a while."

I roll my eyes. "Do we need to tell everyone my life story within two minutes of meeting them?" She turns to me and says, "You should have heard what she told the taxi driver. Did he really need to know how old I was when I learned to walk?"

"It's such a coincidence that you would go on a cruise on the same boat I'm working on," Isabelle says to us.

"It's no coincidence, dear. The universe told me your love life is at a crossroads." Celeste loops her hand through Isabelle's arm. "I'm here to help."

Isabelle gulps. "Um, okay."

I feel sorry for the girl, but relieved that Aunt Celeste has someone new to focus on. My relief is short-lived when my aunt turns to me. "Your love life is at a crossroads, too."

"More like a dead end," I mutter.

"Did you bring your rose quartz crystal with you?" Aunt Celeste asks.

I nod. "It's in my purse."

"Good. I think you'll benefit from its energy."

Isabelle gives us a quizzical look, then excuses herself. "I have to get back to work, but I'll catch up with you guys later."

After we check in, I ask my aunt why she told

Isabelle that Athena was the reason why I wanted to get away from Gáidaros. "You know, it was because of Xander."

Aunt Celeste squeezes my hand. "I didn't think you'd want to talk to a complete stranger about what happened between you and Xander."

"Thanks, I appreciate that," I say. "I'd prefer not to think about him at all."

"Easier said than done," my aunt says.

I take a deep breath. "Isn't that the truth."

* * *

Later that evening, my aunt and I go to the lounge. Within minutes, Aunt Celeste is perched atop the baby grand piano, belting out show tunes to everyone's delight. As I watch her, I wish for the millionth time that I wasn't so tone deaf. Not that I'd get up and perform in front of complete strangers like my aunt. But, still, it'd be nice to be able to sing in the shower without cringing at how off-key I am.

While I'm listening to a particularly spirited rendition of "Take Me or Leave Me" from Rent, a creepy guy walks over and tries to hit on me. When I tell him to get lost, he doesn't take the hint, instead asking if he can get me another drink.

"I can get my own drink, thank you," I say. "Now, if you don't mind, I'm trying to listen to this song."

He looks down at his empty glass. "I need a refill.

I'll be back in a minute."

"Don't bother," I call out. When I see Isabelle walk into the lounge, I wave her over.

"See that guy at the bar? The one with the red hair?" I ask as she sits down. "He keeps trying to hit on me. I've told him repeatedly that I'm not interested, but the message doesn't seem to be getting through."

When I glance back at the bar, Mr. Redhead grins as he raises his glass at me. I shudder. "Switch places with me, will you?" I ask Isabelle.

"Did you tell him you have a boyfriend?" she asks.

"I shouldn't need to mention a boyfriend," I say. "If you tell a guy that you're not interested, that should be enough. There shouldn't have to be another man in the picture to get him to back off."

As I sip my wine, part of me wants to confide in Isabelle about Xander. I tried calling Jasmine, but she's currently on tour somewhere with horrible cell phone reception. I take another sip of wine and surprise myself by saying, "Besides, I'm not sure if I have a boyfriend anymore."

Xander isn't my boyfriend. Xander isn't my anything. Why did I say that?

Isabelle gives me a sympathetic look. "Your aunt mentioned something about his mother. What's going on?"

"Did you ever see *My Big Fat Greek Wedding*? This is kind of like that, but without the wedding. Definitely not the wedding." I stare vacantly out the window, thinking about Athena before turning back to Isabelle. "Xander's mother always envisioned her son marrying a Greek woman. She's constantly playing matchmaker, bringing different girls to his taverna all the time."

"Even when you're there?" I ask.

"Yep. My presence doesn't stop her at all. An American woman, especially one who doesn't even have Greek ancestry, is not what she had planned for her son." I lean forward. "I went to all this trouble learning how to make her favorite dish, but she spent the entire meal pointing out what I did wrong."

"That sounds awful," I say. "What did Xander do?"

"He had a big argument with his mom, but it was in Greek, so I don't know what was said."

"Afterward, he pretended like nothing was wrong, but he became so distant," I say, my eyes welling up as I fudge the truth a bit. Xander became distant, but it wasn't because of his mom. It was because he found out that was working for the Humpty Dumpty corporation the entire time I was on the island.

I take a deep breath, then say, "Anyway, that's when Aunt Celeste suggested this cruise. She thought it would be good for me to get some time away from Xander."

"He'll realize what he's missing," Isabelle says to me. "Absence makes the heart grow fonder."

"But it's not just him. It's like I'm also dating his

family," I say. "Have you ever been in that situation?"

Isabelle shakes her head, then turns to listen to my aunt sing "Bali Ha'i."

"When she was younger, my aunt was in an off-Broadway production of *South Pacific*," I whisper. "It's good to see her so happy. It was hard for her when Uncle Ernie passed away."

When Aunt Celeste finishes, I say, "I love that song. A mysterious island calling to you to come to it—it's so romantic."

"Romantic? How so?" Isabelle asks.

"Did you ever meet someone you fell in love with right away, before you even knew that much about them? That's what it reminds me of—falling for a mysterious stranger and taking a chance on love." I feel my face redden at the saccharine sweet nonsense coming out of my mouth. "I know, I'm being silly. You can't fall in love with someone you know nothing about, right?"

As I take another sip of my wine, it hits me. I've been hiding the real truth from myself. The scary truth. I'm in love with Xander. I toy with my wineglass as I ponder the implications of being brutally honest with myself. Reaching into my purse, I pull out the rose quartz crystal Aunt Celeste gave to me. She told me it would open my heart to love and forgiveness. It's certainly done half of what she promised me—I've admitted to myself that I love

Xander. Now I just need to figure out a way to get him to forgive me.

CHAPTER 16
TACOS FOR THE WIN

During the rest of the riverboat cruise, I focus on two things. The first is easy—I eat amazing food, enjoy the amenities on board, and take part in fabulous shore excursions. Each night, I jot down notes about what I liked and what I didn't like from my perspective as a passenger. The "like" column is way longer than the "didn't like" column. This cruise company could teach Humpty Dumpty a thing or two about making guests feel pampered and special.

The second thing I focus on is a million times more difficult—writing an email to Xander. I want to explain to him why I agreed to be Frank's spy on Gáidaros and why I kept it a secret. My explanation isn't intended to excuse what I did. Nothing can do that. Still, I desperately want Xander to understand the why behind my actions. I want to lay all my flaws on the table as if saying, "Here I am. I'm not perfect. I've made terrible mistakes. But can you love me, anyway?"

Needless to say, I draft countless emails, reread them in disgust, and then hit the delete button. Eventually, I manage to find the right words and, when we reach our last port of call, I hit the send button.

It took a few days and several modes of transportation for my aunt and me to get from Switzerland back to Gáidaros. More than once during our journey, I would turn to Aunt Celeste and tell her that it was foolish for me to try to see Xander again.

"I'll be wasting my time. He'll never forgive me," I would say to her. "He hasn't even responded to my email."

"Nonsense," she would say. "You have to try. If you don't, you'll regret it for the rest of your life."

Now that I'm standing in front of the gate to my aunt's villa, I wonder again why I let her persuade me into coming back here.

"Don't dawdle, dear," my aunt says to me. "You'll want to get freshened up before dinner."

As I follow her into the courtyard, I say, "I'm exhausted from the trip. I might just grab a snack, then go to bed."

"That would be rude," she says.

"Really?" I furrow my brow. "I figured you'd be tired as well."

She shakes her head. "No, not rude to me. Rude to our guest."

I grab my aunt's arm. "Please tell me you didn't invite Xander for dinner. I'm not ready to see him yet."

"Don't worry, dear," she says. "That's not who's coming to dinner."

"I'm confused. If you didn't invite Xander, then who did you invite? It's not like we know a lot of people on this island."

"That's not true. We know lots of folks." Aunt Celeste counts on her fingers as she says, "There's the owner of the bakery, the man who brews that delicious coffee at the kafeneio, the woman who does exquisite embroidery—"

I hold my hand up. "Okay, I'm pretty sure you didn't invite any of them. Spill the beans. Who's coming to dinner tonight? Is it one of the other girls you befriended on your cruise? One of Ginny's friends?"

"Nope."

"This is starting to feel like a game show," I say. "Who's behind door number one?"

"I'll give you a hint," my aunt says. "Her wardrobe consists primarily of black clothes."

My jaw drops. "Oh, my gosh. You invited Athena, didn't you?"

Aunt Celeste chuckles. "The look on your face is priceless."

"This isn't funny," I say. "Athena isn't exactly my biggest fan. She's probably angrier at me than Xander is."

"Why would you say that?"

"Isn't it obvious? Not only did I conceal who my employer was, she knew her son was attracted to me." I tap my chest. "*Me.* A totally inappropriate girl who she fears would lead Xander astray."

My aunt waves a hand in the air, as though dismissing my concerns. "Remember how I told you that Athena might soften up about you, given time?"

"Uh-huh." I tilt my head to one side. "Do you have insider information?"

"Direct from the source." Aunt Celeste grins. "Athena and I have been texting. She sent me the funniest meme the other day. I should show it to you."

I arch an eyebrow. "Sounds like you have a new bestie."

"We have a lot in common. We're both widows, we both like to yodel, and"—my aunt jumps up and down like a little kid—"did I tell you that Athena and I are talking about putting on a little show at the taverna before the end of the summer? I'm going to do some of my favorite show tunes, and she's going to perform some traditional Greek dances."

"How would I have known that? Until a minute ago, I had no idea that the two of you were such good friends." I take a deep breath. "Can we get back to

Xander, please?"

"Well, when I told Athena about the email you sent to her son, she was surprised at first."

"You told her that I contacted Xander?" My eyes widen. "But that was private."

"Before you overreact, you should know that it's worked in your favor," my aunt says. "Like I said, Athena was initially surprised that you were making an effort to explain your actions. She had assumed that you'd disappear from Xander's life without another word."

"There are times when I wanted to do that," I say. "It would have been easier."

"Exactly. That's what I told Athena."

I look at my aunt warily. "What else did you tell her?"

"Basically, what you said in your email to Xander."

"I wish I had never shown it to you," I mutter.

"My hearing is sharper than you think," she says lightly. "I know I shouldn't have meddled, but I couldn't help myself. You and Xander love each other."

"Xander?" I run my fingers through my hair. "Please tell me you haven't been in contact with him as well."

"No, of course not," my aunt says primly. "I'm not that much of a busybody."

I smile at the expression on her face. "Even busybodies have standards, right?"

She bats at me playfully. "Don't get smart with me, young lady."

"You said that, um—" I pause to clear my throat, then ask in a choked voice, "Xander loves me?"

"He does," my aunt says gently. "He admitted it to his mother."

As this sinks in, I press my hands to my mouth. Then I look at my aunt. "Really?"

"Really," she says firmly. "Now go get ready. Athena is going to be here soon."

* * *

The dinner with Athena turns out to be fun. We got slightly tipsy drinking retsina, then my aunt sang some show tunes and Athena taught me the kalamatianos.

"This is the dance you'll do at your wedding," Athena says to me after I collapse in my chair.

"Like they did at the end of *My Big Fat Greek Wedding*," my aunt chimes in as she refills our glasses.

"I think the two of you are getting way ahead of yourselves. There's no wedding on the horizon." I pause to let out a very unladylike burp, then wave my hands in front of me dramatically. "All there is on the horizon is a big fat nothing. Xander never even read my email. I'm sure he deleted it."

"That's not true, darlin'," Athena says. "He read every word. He even read it aloud to me."

I feel my face grow warm. Athena was most certainly not the target audience for particular passages in that email.

"Don't worry." Athena grins at my discomfort. "Xander didn't read the entire thing to me. He said some parts were private."

When my aunt starts to tell Athena about the slightly racy love letters she sent my Uncle Ernie when he was traveling for work, I put my fingers in my ears. No one wants to know the details of their aunts' and uncles' love lives. Not those details, at least.

Eventually, they take pity on me and change the subject. We talk about a whole range of topics, from the best way to change the oil in your car to why donkeys have different manes than horses. Eventually, Athena announces that it's time for her to leave.

As I walk her out, she turns to me and says, "I've been thinking about my daughter, Persephone."

"I'm sorry I never got a chance to meet her," I say.

Athena bows her head and presses her hands together as if saying a silent prayer. Then she looks back up at me and says, "She made mistakes during her short lifetime. In my grief, I blamed her, I blamed myself, I blamed Demetrius' father . . . all I did was try to lay blame at someone's feet. But I've come to realize that all I have to show for that is a long, cold winter of bitterness."

"Winter eventually fades, and spring brings us new growth and blossoms," I say softly.

"It's taken you to show me the importance of forgiveness. I realize now that it's time to move on to a new season of life." Athena squeezes my hand. "Come to dinner tomorrow night at the taverna."

"But, Xander—"

Athena shushes me. "Let me worry about that, darlin'."

* * *

The next night, I walk from the villa to the taverna clutching a tray. My palms are sweating so much that I'm afraid it's going to slip out of my hands. I grasp the sides of the tray tighter. I've worked too long and too hard on making this surprise to have it land on the ground.

As I cross the plaza, I hear a plaintive bleating. I stop in my tracks and look around. "Houdini, is that you?"

The goat comes barreling toward me out of nowhere, almost knocking me into the marble fountain.

"Whoa, little fellow," I say as I steady myself. "Where've you been? I haven't seen you in ages."

Houdini bleats, most likely saying, "Me? I've been here on this island this whole time. Where have you been?"

"I went on a little cruise. Have you ever been to the Rhine River? It's beautiful." When my little goat friend tilts his head to one side, I say, "Sorry, of course you haven't. It's not like you have a passport."

Houdini nods his head up and down at the injustice of the authorities not issuing travel documentation to animals, then proceeds to chew on the bottom of my skirt.

"Stop it. I want to look nice for Xander." I hold the tray closer to my chest. "If you behave, I'll bring you back a doggy bag from dinner. Or rather, a goat bag."

Houdini bleats in response, then wanders off to drink out of the fountain.

I take a deep breath, then exhale slowly. When I've gathered my nerve, I traverse the rest of the way to the taverna. I push open the door, but instead of being greeted by the usual noise and bustle of folks chatting away over their meals, the place is deadly silent. It isn't my birthday, so I'm not expecting a surprise party, but I still glance around warily for people waiting to jump out and give me a heart attack.

That's when I notice tea lights on the floor. They're arranged in such a manner that they create a pathway leading out to the terrace. I'm frozen in place with indecision. Do I follow the flickering lights or do I turn tail and run back to the villa?

The smell of something familiar wafts through the dining room, jolting me into action. I have to know if that's what I think it is. Holding the tray close to my chest as though it's some sort of symbolic armor, I walk out onto the terrace with more confidence than I feel.

When I see what's laid out on one of the tables, I nearly faint from disbelief. "Is that a taco bar?" I splutter.

"It sure is, complete with a choice of soft or crunchy taco shells and all the fixings," someone mysterious says in a deep voice.

Who am I kidding? There's no mystery about who replied to me. Of course, it's Xander. But I can't bear to make eye contact with him. If I did, what would I see? Would his dark eyes be cold and angry or would they be warm and welcoming? I focus on the array of salsas instead.

"Aren't you going to say anything, Olivia?" Xander asks.

"I thought you hated tacos," I say, shifting my gaze to the bowls of guacamole, chopped tomatoes, and shredded lettuce.

"That's not exactly true. I hate what they reminded me of," Xander says. "Persephone loved tacos."

"She did?" My eyes flicker upward briefly, but then I quickly look back down. The crunchy taco shells look like they just came out of the deep fryer.

"Chicken with salsa verde and extra sour cream was her favorite."

"That sounds like a good combination," I say.

"I wish you could have met her," Xander says wistfully. "She would have liked eating tacos with you."

I shift the tray in my hands. "Is that why you got a taco tattoo? As a reminder of her?"

Xander doesn't say anything for the longest time. When he finally does, the pain in his voice breaks my heart. "I miss her so much."

I look up sharply and see tears streaming down Xander's face. He locks his eyes with mine, then nods slowly. Instinctively knowing what he needs, I rush over and pull him into my arms, dropping the tray in the process. We embrace for a while, then I stroke the side of his face and whisper, "I'm sorry."

"Um, why is your hand sticky?" Xander asks after a beat.

I pull my hand away and groan. "Those stupid bees."

Xander laughs. "What are you talking about?"

"There," I say, pointing at the mess on the floor. "I made baklava. The honey got all over me when I dropped the tray."

He squats down and scoops the ruined baklava back onto the tray. "At least it's not burnt this time. That seems like a good sign."

"Is it?" I ask. "Do you think things can work out with us?"

Xander sets the tray down on a table, then hands

me a napkin. While we wipe honey off our hands, he says, "I have to be honest. I was so angry with you at first."

"Then what happened?"

He fishes something out of his pocket and holds it up. "This happened."

"Is that rose quartz?"

"Your aunt gave it to me. She told me to keep it close to me at all times. I thought it was kind of a strange gift, but your aunt is um . . ."

"Persistent and eccentric," I suggest. When Xander nods, I say, "My aunt gave me one as well. She said rose quartz is good for opening yourself to love and forgiveness."

Xander gives me a wry smile. "That's exactly what happened. When I initially got your email, I wasn't sure what to think. But my mother, of all people, told me some people are worth second chances. I ignored her advice, but it was like this crystal was calling to me. I'd swear I put in a drawer, but then I'd find it under my pillow. If it was in my pocket, it felt like it was burning my skin. It wasn't until I admitted to myself that I couldn't live without you that it left me in peace."

"Does that mean you forgive me?" I ask quietly.

"I do," he says simply. "Now what?"

The weight of the moment feels heavy, scary almost, so I lighten the mood. "I have two burning questions."

"Only two?" he asks.

"Two for now," I say. "I reserve the right to ask future questions."

"Okay, what's the first one?"

"Do you like crunchy or soft tacos?"

Xander pretends to think about it for a moment, then says, "Crunchy."

"Good answer," I say with a grin.

"What's the second question? Am I going to need a calculator?"

I shake my head. "Before I ask it, do you remember the bet we made?"

"That you couldn't guess what my favorite TV show was? Sure, I remember it."

"Well, I know what the answer is."

He chuckles. "Not a chance."

"Don't give me that cocky smile."

He puts a hand to his chest in mock horror. "Me? Cocky smile?"

"It's one of the things I love about you. Although your unibrow comes in a close second."

Xander's cocky grin disappears. He stares at me in stunned silence. Then he takes my hand in his, intertwining our fingers together. "Did you say you love me?" he asks softly.

"I also said you had a unibrow," I point out.

"We'll get back to that in a moment." Xander bites back a smile, then lifts my hand to his lips. After kissing it gently, he asks, "Do you love me?"

"Yes." After I utter that one simple word, I wait for a response. Preferably a response like, "I love you too." But, honestly, after you put your heart on the line, any response will do. Anything is better than a long, unbearable stretch of silence.

Finally, Xander says something in Greek.

I'm clueless. Based on the fact that Xander has a shy smile on his face and that he's still holding my hand, I don't think he said, "Can we just be friends," in Greek. At least I hope he didn't. Aunt Celeste told me that Xander was in love with me, but I need to hear it from him.

I take a deep breath, then ask, "Do you mind translating that, please?"

With that same shy smile, he says, "It means, 'I love you.'"

I lean in to kiss him, but he pulls away. "Not so fast. What's my favorite TV show?"

"*Firefly*," I say smugly. "Which leads me to my second question—tell me why you like that show."

"Because it's a mash-up of two different genres—westerns and science fiction," Xander says.

"They don't sound like they go together."

"You'd think that, right? But, somehow it works. Kind of like how two people from two different backgrounds can complement each other."

"Good answer." I try to suppress my smile. "Now give me my reward."

"There's no way you could have guessed that on

your own." Xander shakes his head. "You cheated. I don't know how, but you cheated."

"Sounds like someone's a sore—" I start to say, but Xander silences me with a kiss. As his lips press against mine, someone clears their throat. I reluctantly pull away from Xander and turn around.

Athena is standing there, her arms folded across her chest. "Save that for after you're married," she says gruffly.

"Maybe we should listen to the lady," Xander whispers in my ear before kissing me again.

EPILOGUE – XANDER
(FOUR YEARS LATER)

"Checkmate," my father-in-law says triumphantly.

"Again, Jim?" I survey the chessboard in dismay, trying to figure out where I went wrong.

"Want some scotch, Xander?" He pats me on my back. "Might take the sting out of your defeat. Isn't that the fourth chess match you've lost in a row?"

I smile. "It's three, but who's counting?"

While Jim pours our drinks, I walk over to the bay window and look outside. My in-laws live in Minnesota, so you'd think you're pretty much guaranteed a white Christmas. But when Olivia and I flew in from Greece earlier in the week, they were forecasting rain over the holidays. She had been so disappointed. In her mind, it's not Christmas unless you can make snowmen and go sledding. Thankfully, the rain has turned into snow, and it's coming down fast and furious.

"Thanks," I say when Jim hands me my drink. After taking an appreciative sip, I ask, "What's happened to the girls?"

"I think Olivia and her mom are wrapping presents." My father-in-law points at large, oddly shaped package under the Christmas tree. "That one is from Celeste. She gives me the strangest presents. Last year it was a cutting board with Nicholas Cage's face on it. Go figure."

"What's she up to now?" I ask.

"Last I heard, she was backpacking through Thailand with her new husband. She's on a quest to learn how to make the perfect pad thai." He inspects the present from Celeste, trying to figure out what the tubular protrusion sticking out of the front is. After giving up, he asks, "How's your mom doing?"

"Great," I say. "The cooking school she opened is going really well. She's fully booked through next summer."

"She's not concerned that will mean more tourists on Gáidaros?" he asks.

"No, my mom and Olivia have worked really hard together on making sure that the tourism on the island is sustainable. It's managed very carefully so that it benefits our local economy, but without destroying the essence of what makes Gáidaros so special," I say. "You two really need to come back for a visit."

"Cathy was just saying that to me this morning," Jim says. "She thinks we should take a trip there at the end of this summer."

"That would be perfect. You can celebrate—"

Olivia comes up behind me and puts her arm around my waist. "What are we celebrating?"

I kiss the top of her head. "Our third wedding anniversary."

"Maybe we'll be celebrating more than that," Cathy says as she sets some gift-wrapped presents under the tree.

"Like what?" I ask.

My mother-in-law and Olivia exchange glances, then Olivia rushes out of the room.

"Are you okay?" I call out after her.

"She'll be fine." Cathy pats my arm, then asks if I want any cocoa. "I have those tiny marshmallows you like."

"Cocoa sounds good," I say.

She grabs our empty scotch glasses, then bustles off to the kitchen while Jim stokes the fire. After a few minutes, Cathy returns with the cocoa and a tray of baked goods.

I grin at my mother-in-law. "Your famous cardamom spice cookies. If Olivia doesn't hurry back, there might not be any left."

While I'm eating my third cookie, Olivia walks into the living room, clutching a present to her chest.

"Here, I can put that under the tree for you," I say

as she sits next to me. "Is it for your mom or dad?"

"It's actually for you." She hands me the present, then laughs as she brushes a few cookie crumbs off my shirt. "How many of these have you had?"

"You better grab one while you can," I say.

"They're all yours," Olivia says before pressing her hand to her mouth.

"Hey, are you okay?" I ask. "You look like you're going to be sick."

Jim frowns. "I hope you didn't pick up a tummy bug."

"She'll be fine," Cathy reassures my father-in-law. Then she turns to Olivia. "Now might be a good time for Xander to open his present, don't you think?"

"But I thought we agreed that we'd exchange gifts on Christmas morning," I say.

Olivia squeezes my hand. "I think we should make an exception for this one."

"Go on," Cathy urges me.

I look back and forth between Olivia and her mother, wondering what they're up to. Then I tear off the wrapping paper. As I lift the lid off the box, Cathy claps her hands together and squeals.

Olivia grins. "Try to contain yourself, Mom."

After digging through the tissue paper, I pull out my present and hold it up for everyone to see.

Jim peers over his reading glasses. "Is that some sort of dishcloth? What's that strange pattern on it?"

"It's tacos, Dad," Olivia says. "Tiny dancing tacos."

"Huh, dancing tacos. That's odd. Seems like something your Aunt Celeste would buy."

Cathy nudges her husband. "For goodness' sake, Jim. It's not a dishtowel."

"Well then, what is it?" my father-in-law asks as he leans forward for a better look.

I feel the blood draining from my face as the realization of what I'm holding in my hands represents. After I clear my throat, I say softly, "It's a onesie."

"But isn't that what you dress a baby in?" Jim asks.

Olivia rubs my arm. "Now, you're the one who looks faint."

"Is it true?" I ask. "Are you pregnant?"

"I sure am." Her blue eyes sparkle. "We're going to have a baby this summer."

As I pull Olivia into an embrace, I say, "This is the best present ever."

"Aren't you glad you didn't wait until Christmas morning to open it?" She kisses me lightly, then whispers, "If it's a girl, I think we should name her Persephone."

And just like that, when I think I couldn't love my wife more, she proves me wrong once again.

AUTHOR'S NOTE

Thank you so much for reading *Smitten with Baklava*. If you enjoyed it, I'd be grateful if you would consider leaving a short review on Goodreads and/or your favorite retailer. Reviews help other readers find my books and encourage me to keep writing.

My husband and I have been lucky enough to visit Greece a few times and our travels there were the inspiration for this book. Unlike Olivia, I'm not an overly picky eater and practically ate my way through our Greek travels.

It's always a bit of a torture writing my Smitten with Travel romantic comedies because all I do is think about the delicious foods I've sampled in other countries. It's possible I may have even drooled a little bit on my keyboard while writing about spanakopita, dolmades, baklava . . . Um, we're going to have to pause this author's note for a few minutes while I go get a snack.

Okay, I'm back now (she says, wiping crumbs off her shirt). When my doctor asks me why I've gained so much weight, I'm going to blame these books.

Anyway, before I go, I want to give a shout-out to my editor, Beth Balmanno at By the Books Editing. She's thorough, flexible, and easy to work with. And, as always, a huge thank you to my husband. His support means the world to me.

If you'd like to know when I have a new release, find out about sales/promos, and get other updates, you can sign up for my newsletter to stay in touch: https://www.subscribepage.com/m4g9m4

ABOUT THE AUTHOR

Ellen Jacobson is a chocolate obsessed cat lover who writes cozy mysteries and romantic comedies. After working in Scotland and New Zealand for several years, she returned to the States, lived aboard a sailboat, traveled around in a tiny camper, and is now settled in a small town in northern Oregon with her husband and an imaginary cat named Simon.

Find out more at ellenjacobsonauthor.com

ALSO BY ELLEN JACOBSON

Smitten with Travel Romantic Comedies

Smitten with Ravioli
Smitten with Croissants
Smitten with Strudel
Smitten with Candy Canes
Smitten with Baklava

Mollie McGhie Mysteries

Robbery at the Roller Derby
Murder at the Marina
Bodies in the Boatyard
Poisoned by the Pier
Buried by the Beach
Dead in the Dinghy
Shooting by the Sea
Overboard on the Ocean
Murder Aboard the Mistletoe

North Dakota Library Mysteries

Planning for Murder

Made in the USA
Monee, IL
03 July 2023

38585975R00132